A Lot Like Love...

A Li'l Like Chocolate

SUMRIT SHAHI

Published by
Rupa Publications India Pvt. Ltd 2017
7/16, Ansari Road, Daryaganj
New Delhi 110002

Sales Centres:
Allahabad Bengaluru Chennai
Hyderabad Jaipur Kathmandu
Kolkata Mumbai

Copyright © Sumrit Shahi 2011, 2017

This is a work of fiction. Names, characters, places and incidents are either the product of the author's imagination or are used fictitiously and any resemblance to any actual person, living or dead, events, or
locales is entirely coincidental.

All rights reserved.

No part of this publication may be reproduced, transmitted,
or stored in a retrieval system, in any form or by any means,
electronic, mechanical, photocopying, recording or otherwise,
without the prior permission of the publisher.

ISBN: 978-81-291-4838-4

First impression 2017

10 9 8 7 6 5 4 3 2 1

The moral right of the author has been asserted.

Printed in India by Nutech Print Services, New Delhi

This book is sold subject to the condition that it shall not,
by way of trade or otherwise, be lent, resold, hired out, or otherwise circulated,
without the publisher's prior consent, in any form of binding or cover other than
that in which it is published.

*Indebted to His Holiness Hardev Singh Ji Maharaj,
the reason for my existence and the guardian
of light in this dark world.*

Dedicated to Anandi Gulati.
'If you're alone, I'll be your shadow. If you want to cry, I'll be your shoulder. If you want a hug, I'll be your pillow. If you need to be happy, I'll be your smile. But, anytime you need a friend, I'll just be me.'
*That was her. The best friend you could desire. She's a star today, up there. I may not see her, but she's with me.
Always.*

Ek tuhi Nirankar
Mein teri sharan han
Mainu baksh lo

one

And that's how it began…or…ummm…perhaps…ended!

27 May 2010

'So…are you sure, you want to do this?'

'Yyess…yes!'

'Nervous?'

'A little.'

'We could do this later…I mean, when you're comfortable with the idea.'

'No…this had to happen anyway. So, can we just get over with this quickly, now?'

'We could go back to my place and do it…it'll be easier…it's just seven in the morning…sneaking in won't be an issue.'

'Shadab, stop being the princess in the situation! The car is comfortable enough.'

The tension in the air-conditioned black Ford Endeavour, with equally black-tinted glasses and folded back seats, standing in the secluded parking lot of their gym, is overwhelming.

He takes a deep breath and reaches for his shorts.

She closes her eyes in anticipation.

'Did you open it?' Her voice is a whisper.

His fingers work faster than the internet on his mobile and finally it loads.

www.cbse.nic.in

Shadab and Arnika.
Both seventeen.
In love. Well, something like that.
In the most crucial act of their lives.

Yes, the Board results. They weren't supposed to be out till next evening but apparently CBSE had got an early hand on and it couldn't stop itself from screwing the odd million lives associated with the declaration of the Class XII results.

Shadab, a little shy of six feet, a lot more proud of his length, a natural athletic frame with just the right cut here and sculpted muscle there, a light shade of a stubble, a darker mop of curly hair (on the head!), had been pumping the iron while Arnika, with a slender, firm and muscular frame of five feet and six inches, angular features, a poker-straight ponytail, some acceptable piercings, oodles of attitude, truckload of practicality, was busy doing the cardio, when her cell phone beeped. Two minutes later, the whole gym heard what seemed like 'a woman in labour' shriek.

In panic, pain, pressure, they had rushed down to his car.
This was it!
Their future.
Their career.
THEM.

It had begun just like any other normal day.

5.40 a.m.
Arnika's alarm starts vibrating in her ear.

5.42 a.m.
She finally opens her eyes on realizing that the vibrations are for real.

5.43 a.m.
She presses 2 on her speed dial. *Shadab*, the name flashes on the screen. Speed dial 1 is for her mother. Priorities!

5.47 a.m.
He finally answers on the fifth try.

5.50 a.m.
She finishes shouting at him for not picking up the four calls.

5.52 a.m.
He gets out of bed and looks around for his clothes.

5.53 a.m.
She accuses him of watching porn late into the night and falling asleep naked.

5.54 a.m.
He denies it, still searching for his shorts.

5.55 a.m.
She instructs him to look for them under the sheets.

5.56 a.m.
They both grin after he finds them just there!

5.58 a.m.
He goes to the washroom with the cell phone stuck to his ear, applies casual strokes of the toothbrush up and down and does a very quick gargle. A rushed spray of deodorant and a tinge of aftershave. *'Yes I'm ready,'* he proclaims.

5.59 a.m.
'Err...I'll get some gum,' she says and ends the call.

6.04 a.m.
He drives his SUV at full speed, taking advantage of the empty Chandigarh roads. Technically underage, his rich, loving and questionably responsible parents know he won't screw with the car, not because he's a victim of authority but because he loves the motor machine more than the man who paid for it and the mother who coaxed her husband to let their son drive.

Some five kilometres, three signal jumps, sizeable moments of rash driving and two wrong turns later, he reaches her house.

Honks once. Honks twice. Honks again.

She knows he's there but she won't come out. It's more like revenge being best served early morning and cold.

He honks yet again.

She opens the main door by an eyebrow fraction just to see if her old neighbour has been disturbed enough from his daily yoga routine to come out and shout at him.

6.09 a.m.
Seeing that her neighbour is done with his daily curses, she finally opens the main door, runs till the main gate in her shorts and gym tee and pretends to be sorry for being late.

He knows she's pretending. The last five minutes of the verbal duel with the old neighbour are worth the twinkle in her eye.

6.15 a.m.
They both reach the almost-empty gym parking.

6.16 a.m.
It's time for some tonsil tennis (not before using the chewing gum though!).

That night… that very night of celebrations… cerebral decisions and champagne… loads of it.

Pop!

The champagne bottle lives up to its stereotype of all things celebratory.

Everybody is drenched in sweat and alcohol. It's 10 p.m. The party has been on for two hours now.

There's been enough of dancing to the powerful Bose dock speakers and doctored playlists, playing different songs.

Most of the girls are cursing themselves silently for wearing tops tight enough to suffocate their food pipes and dresses short enough to cause scandals.

Some odd fifty-sixty Class XII students of J.W.S. High School, one of the premier institutions of the city, have been invited for Shadab's party at his farmhouse, on the outskirts of the city—a farmhouse, very typical one with a large swimming pool, lonely old caretakers, a lot of open space and complete privacy from parents.

Outside is a line-up of cars, glamorous enough to organize a mini-auto show. Bored drivers group together to bitch about the rich, spoilt kids.

Inside, nobody is ready to wait for the glasses. The bottles are being passed around and everybody is standing in clusters, some swaying to the music, some swaying from the additional mix of excessive breezers and cold snacks, while some, sitting in the corner, are romancing the *sheesha* and some simply standing and laughing, for it so happens that one of the corks has flown aimlessly but with determination to land among a pair of hills. *Safely but painfully.*

'Ouch,' Rhea screams, trying hard but failing miserably to inconspicuously adjust her tube top and relieve it of the sudden corky pain. *The babe for the guys, the bitch for the girls*, causing hand aches and heartaches with equal aplomb, is the snob every school boasts off.

Her little explosive and extremely talked-about tryst with Shadab is a thing of the past, that is, before Arnika joined the school. By natural consequence, the ladies don't gel—and how!

She's got a 76 per cent—good enough for her Daddy to send his little princess to London for a fairy tale fashion-designing course.

'Sorry,' Ritesh, being the gentleman that he is, walks up sheepishly to her and apologizes.

He's not good with popping…champagnes, of course!

He has finished commerce with 89 per cent, promising enough for a private college BBA; close enough to Alisha.

Shadab has been his best friend since the time of trading tiffin boxes, then computer games followed by PlayStation, CDs gradually progressing to porno and *Playboy* magazines.

'Don't pay the bitch any heed,' Alisha whispers in his ear over the loud music after Rhea snubs him.

Alisha, the sorted one, the scandal-less and an SRCC candidate, was Ritesh's girlfriend and Shadab's 4 a.m.-advice friend. Straightforward, simple and sleek, known to speak her mind and offer sound advice, she's been the reason Shadab and Arnika have never fought for more than a week (that too when she had been out of the country and Skype really wasn't an option).

Vasu, Sudhir and Bani—that completes the group.

FRIENDS.

They've been infamously together for bunking classes, to fights for water at the water cooler, to playing hide and seek and hiding in the principal's office, to playing 'tear the pocket' and hanging out virtually every day.

Suddenly somebody changed the song—'*Yaroon dosti badi hi haseen hai...*'

The background music changed to solemn gears and so did the atmosphere. School has officially ended. Everybody is gearing up to walk a new lonely road—a road that leads to college, to new opportunities, to a new life.

Some ten minutes later...

The seven friends sit together in a secluded corner with breezers in every hand. Arnika's head rests on Shadab's shoulder; Bani animatedly stares into the night sky; Sudhir, a little high, a little contemplative, whistles; Vasu fidgets with his cell without a cause and Alisha unnaturally talks at a rate Ritesh has never witnessed before.

'So this is it, people!' Shadab says, gulping a large sip from his bottle and ending on a soft note.

'This is it? I thought we had some more booze stocked up,' Vasu says innocently and everybody starts laughing.

'What's that on your neck?' Bani suddenly asks Shadab.

'What?' he questions as Arnika also gets up in a reflex.

'The propped-up collar trick mister...Arni...when did you both exactly reach the farm for the preparations?' she enquires as everyone starts to smile.

'Well...ummm...you know...,' Arnika looks at Shadab.

His cue. 'Oh c'mon...it's just you know...our symbol of being together,' he ends.

'Together...and aggressive,' Ritesh chips in.

They all laugh.
Aggression. True!
Passion. True.
Practicality. True.

Arnika had kept a *'no-touch, not-much clause'* for them ever since the Boards had started. The agreement has now expired.

'You both look so cute together...how would you survive without each other?' Alisha says to the other couple, ending their laughter.

There is sudden silence.

Both of them are quiet—the boy content, stroking her hair, and the girl considerate yet determined, feeling secure in his arms.

The couple—Shadab and Arnika.

Bachelors of Theatre Arts, Hansraj College (University of Delhi) and National School of Drama

Shadab's 92 per cent in Humanities, an undying passion for theatre, being president of the school theatre and debating club, guarantees him admission to his dream college—a dream he had envisaged much before Arnika had come into his life and love had beckoned.

President George Institute for International Law and Public Relations, New York

Arnika's 95 per cent in Humanities, a remarkable SAT score, a keen interest in debating and International Relations and Law—all worked in her favour to help her achieve her dream—a dream which had inhabited her heart before Shadab encroached on it.

'We'll make this work,' she says softly.
'We will,' he replies.

Two different countries.
Two hearts.
Two time zones.
Trust.
Trials.
The next song on the playlist is heard: *'Yeh dooriyan...'*

So...love...eh?

Love. A pristine feeling. It's the freshness of morning dew—fragile yet beautiful. It's like an iPod with your favourite playlist on repeat mode. It's like a painter's first stroke—vulnerable, unsure yet intense. It is the uncertainty of the Indian monsoon. It is like the thrill of having a *burf ka gola* on a chilly December night. It is as unpredictable as the stock market. It is as dependable as your LIC policy. It is as sweet and crooked as a deep-fried *jalebi*. It is noisier than the Delhi traffic, quieter than the sea at night. It is more demanding than your Board exams, more challenging than the AIEEE or the CAT. It can get dirtier than a teenager's bedroom. It can be as painful as the first period. It is whiter than pearls, more twisted than a salon-returned girl's curls. It gives a glow, shinier than bleach. It's naughtier than a boy and girl together on a secluded beach. It is more addictive than coffee, crispier than KFC, deadlier than an LSD trip. It's the nervousness of the first kiss or the tension of a period miss.

A lot like love happened to them...just when they met a year ago...

two

And that's how they met…not the perfect setting but yeah…

4 May 2009

8.20 a.m.
'Arnika Sinha,' she repeats her name for the school receptionist, after she's reached late on the first day of her new school. Not her virtue. But it wasn't her fault. A mother on the driving seat and a city not yet explored. Women and roads. Bumpy connections.

It's a new beginning for her—one that brought an end to her stay in Gurgaon and transported her to Chandigarh. A beginning where she's been uprooted from the garden of her old city, her old friends, her life. A beginning where she is suddenly expected to germinate herself in Class XII, in a new school, just when cliques are already set, groups already made.

Getting admission in J.W.S. High School hasn't been tough. Having a celebrated national theatre artist and bestselling author as a mother, a glorious academic record, some debating wins and community service certificates help, plus India is all about pulling the right strings at the right places. Admission had been soft music.

'New admission?' the surprisingly young receptionist enquires yet again.

'Yes ma'am,' she replies, trying her best to sound polite. She looks at the large clock in the school office; she definitely should be in class.

'Okay...so?' the right-out-of-college receptionist questions while fidgeting with her mobile phone.

So, garland me, bitch. 'I was told by the coordinator to report here.'

The receptionist giggles after reading a newly received SMS. It's from her boyfriend. The giggle is such a giveaway.

Ugh...love! Arnika cringes her nose at the very thought of such claustrophobic expression of emotion.

'Excuse me, ma'am...if you could talk to your boyfriend later?'

She's like that. Fearless. Bold. Outspoken.

The receptionist is simply taken aback. She's, with much surety, not prone to such poker replies. The school phone rings, leaving no time for her to retort.

'J.W.S. High School,' her voice is purely mechanical.

'Yyess...Ggood Mmorning Principal ma'am...the new girl,' she looks at Arnika. 'Yyess...she's there...okay,' she places the receiver back. 'Ma'am is calling you to her room,' she says, coldly pointing towards the door on the extreme right.

Arnika walks up to the door and knocks on it. She opens the door carefully after hearing a muffled, 'Come in'.

'Arnika...come in,' she recognizes the principal's voice immediately from their last and only meeting. 'Good morning... Come, have a seat.'

'Morning ma'am,' Arnika chirps, adjusting the new school skirt as she sits on the chair, scissor legged.

'Arnika...welcome to J.W.S. How pretty you look in the school uniform and these flicks...how beautiful.'

'Thank you, ma'am,' Arnika smiles back.

'If only, child, you could button up your shirt, pin up your hair and not wear nail paint or any piece of jewellery from tomorrow... I'm sure you will have a great time here,' she pauses to flash an acidic smile. 'You see, Arnika, we are very particular about school rules here... about appearance...values...ethics...virtues such as punctuality...'

'But, I...,' Arnika's voice cuts midway.

'I know... it's your first day but I'd expected you to be here at 8 a.m... I'd told your mother how particular and popular our school is about discipline and order.'

Bang!!! Suddenly the door opens and a muscular man in a sports suit, which Arnika presumes correctly to be the P.E. Teacher, walks in, followed by a boy.

'Ma'am...he was smoking in the squash court and when the guard saw him...he bribed him and sent him away... I just happened to go inside and smelt smoke... It turned out to be him, merrily listening to music on his MP3 player.'

'It's an iPod sir...not an MP3 player and that wasn't me smoking...the guard had just left two minutes ago... Check his pockets, you'll find the cigarettes...' the boy murmurs with confidence.

A giggle escapes Arnika's mouth. She covers her face, not looking at the boy.

The teacher in the next instant realizes that the principal is not alone and begins to apologize for barging in. 'I thought you were alone...the receptionist also did not stop me.'

The principal takes a deep breath, adjusts her spectacles, composes herself and raises her hand, indicating the boy to stand adjacent to her table.

'First you were caught bunking,' the principal begins, forgetting that Arnika is still sitting there. 'Then you used the fire extinguisher on one of your classmates...then you were caught playing food fight in the home science lab...you're the president of the debating and theatre club…you know, you're a student I can't think of losing…then, why do you force me to change my opinion…why?'

Debating. This is her field, her future. Her area of interest. She turns her head to give the boy a proper scan. Connections help.

'Shadab…answer me,' the principal demands, pleadingly.

The boy who has kept his gaze on the Italian tiled floor till now, suddenly looks up on his name being called.

'I'm sorry,' he blurts, for the first time without much resistance, as his gaze collides with the gaze of the girl sitting there. He's never seen her before; in fact, he's never seen any of her kind before.

Natural, slender and beautiful—even in the school uniform. Something rises somewhere. Below the belt.

She's hot. They both are aware of it. Arnika passes him a faint smile. Very faint, enough for him to notice though.

He's cute. But not killing cute. It's not like she cares anyway. Debating president. That's all that matters. She knows she would have smiled even if he had been a cross between an elephant and a monkey.

If you have it, flaunt it. Her smile is killer. And she loves playing the assassin.

'You won't get away with a "sorry" this time…I want to meet your father tomorrow afternoon,' the principal continues.

'Okay,' he replies, indifferently. Acting cool is just a preposition for the player.

'Well…Mr Pandey…you may leave then,' the principal instructs the P.E. Teacher and he complies. She is about to begin again but is cut short by her mobile's ringtone.

'I need to take this,' she murmurs under her breath and picks the call.

Meanwhile...

Shadab's trying hard to not look at her.

She's doing just the same.

He knows it. It's a guy thing.

'Yes Mr Sharma...could you just hold on for a moment,' the principal covers her cell with her fat, sweaty hand and says, 'okay now, go back to your class...quickly...and yes, Arnika...he'll guide you...Shadab meet your new classmate,' the call is resumed.

'Hi!' Shadab smiles.

'Hey!' She smiles back.

And for the first time in the history of mankind...a school principal sets the stage for a love story (of course, unknowingly).

And it's not over...not without the walk to remember...till the class, that is!

'So first day...are you nervous?'

He has a deep voice, deep enough to turn her on, she realizes as he literally takes the lead and shows her the way to her class.

'For the others...a little.'

'Hot. Witty. It's a royal combo,' he concludes as he continues to walk casually, ahead, ensuring there is enough distance between them for her to scan his gym-fed butt.

He's worn his briefs today. Briefs which make the butt look even more firm.

She graces 'it' with a look. Like any other girl would. A quick and secret lusty look.

Next, she shifts her view to the students sitting in the various classrooms, as she passes them.

Long hair, low waists, rolled up sleeves—for the guys; open shirt buttons, folded skirts, carefully done careless hairdo—for the girls. Groups at the water cooler—the guys filling in the bottles while the girls giggle.

This comforts her. The principal is a hoax. The school seems to be high on rule breaking.

'So, where are you from?' He asks the simplest question after a few silent seconds, just to keep the conversation in motion. Class XII, Humanities block stands in the extreme right corner of the school premises. Distance does the trick.

'Gurgaon,' she repeats, adjusting her skirt again.

'Nice…there isn't anything better than Blu-O at Ambience Mall!' he exclaims.

'Yes dude, you've been there, every tourist has,' she says in her head.

'Do you mind if we go to the library first? I really need to get this book,' he questions, still walking a few steps ahead.

'Umm…okay,' she agrees, looking at him from behind, once again.

Athletic build, struggling school pants, firm butt, spiked hair…he doesn't really seem the library-going guy…'is he trying to impress me?' she wonders.

He takes a left, climbs up a flight of stairs as she follows. 'Damn…it's closed!' He exclaims, holding the lock in his hand, after they reach the senior library. 'The librarian is such a bummer,' he continues.

'Not more than the receptionist here,' she says with some air in her words.

His little flesh on the cheeks takes a semicircular arc in no time. 'Well, let's just say…she's dedicated to her cell phone,' he concludes.

'Ahh yes!' It's her turn to exclaim. 'By the way, which book did you want from the library?' she continues as they begin to walk back, this time by a different route.

'I've been searching for this book forever and the librarian had promised to get it today…it's a limited edition…hardly available.'

'Which one?'

He's got her interested; he knows, she knows.

'*The Theatrical Lies* by…'

'Nishi Sinha,' she completes the information for him.

'Wow…are you also into theatre?'

'Not much…but let's just say I've lived with it all my life.'

'I didn't get that.'

'Nothing…I have the book at home…I could get it for you… an author-signed copy.'

'You must be joking…Nishi Sinha's signature…dude, I idolize that woman…she's just so…'

'Difficult sometimes,' she murmurs under her breath.

'You said something?'

'No…nothing…hey, but Shabad…'

'It's Shadab.'

'Yeah…the same thing.'

'It's not.'

'Right SHADAB,' she stresses.

He finds it sexy. Her swimsuit figure is not helping the rising issues either.

'Back there in the principal office…you're the debating society president?' she ends the statement more like a question.

'That sounds more like an allegation…dude…I'm just allergic to rules…not a rebel.'

They both laugh.

They aren't exactly walking now; it's more of a casual stroll in the corridors.

'I didn't mean that... I mean... do you have auditions for these societies or it's like anybody can join... because I thrive on public speaking.'

'Auditions? But they happened last month... you've joined late... Class XII... some specific reason?' He knows the fish is in the net.

'Yeah... my grandma is all alone... can't live without my Mom... the empty nest syndrome... no other choice... had to shift.'

'Oh, okay.'

The school bell rings. He looks at his watch. It's a Rado. She isn't the type who'd notice though, he knows it. She's wearing an Omega herself.

'I think we should head to class... the political science teacher has a serious repulsion to latecomers.'

'Sure... but how about you? Have some more mint. The cig's smell... it's a little strong... Marlboro light... unless you can handle it,' she smiles.

He's at a loss for words. This girl knows the sticks. Pretty well.

'Dude... welcome to the debating society... I think you'll be fun to hang out with.'

'Yeah... I hope you don't prove my judgement wrong either.'

He smiles, she smiles, problem solved.

three

*And they go out for their first coffee…in the school uniform…
using the school car.*

5 July 2009

'And the best team of the 11th Vivekananda Annual Debate is Shadab Parvez and Arnika Sinha, J.W.S. High School, Chandigarh.'

A deafening applause engulfs the auditorium of the host school; they have come to participate in the debate.

'Yes!' Arnika and Shadab Hi5 each other as they get up and walk up to the stage to collect their certificates and their team trophy.

Their. Team. All plural. Nothing singular. THEM.

'This had to happen,' Shadab's thoughts bounce in his head. Arnika has been bloody good with her improvised speech—good enough to captivate the entire audience with her command and confidence. He's been just a regular in comparison, good support but nothing extraordinary.

The bored, old chief guest, a local M.P., who is compelled by obligation to go through the proceedings, hands over the trophy and certificates to them. The local newspaper's photographer asks them to step aside for a picture.

'Smile,' he asks both of them to pose in a particular angle and flex their jaws.

Their first picture together. Just them. Both smiling. Different reasons.

School, tuitions, evening get-togethers, early dinners, a month of summer vacations, an odd night sneak out, a few birthday parties. Arnika has found ground, a real rosy and grassy one in these two months. Not that she doesn't miss her friends back in Gurgaon but this city, this school, its people, her classmates, her new-found friends—Bani, Vasu, Alisha, Shadab and the rest—everyone has been just so welcoming. Added to it is the very simple fact that she's killer hot and surprisingly intelligent. Any guy wouldn't even mind getting his balls pierced if it could get him to talk to her, leave alone befriend her.

With such a description at disposal, it's normal that every fifth guy around has thought about her, in the classroom, in the toilet, in the basketball field, at the swimming pool where she goes every evening for a swim, some being single, some despite being committed! And she's been polite enough to courteously kill everybody's rising hopes and pulsating desires with her 'honest' replies and no-nonsense attitude.

Love, commitment—such words have never been a top priority for her; blame it on her parents' separation when she was eleven; blame it on a failed relationship in the past; blame it on her career-oriented mind, she's chosen to stay this way.

Beautiful yet single.

Friendly yet focussed.

Shadab understood this. Theatre helps you to interpret people. He's been there with her but never been all over her. Just a good friend, a debating partner, a person whom she hangs out with in a group, has gone for lunches and movies or to do sheesha.

Not that there haven't been rumour mills about them, blowing gossip at high velocity, but he's been careful—flirting once in a while, getting to know her, trying to understand the gravity of the situation and then work his charms.

A reputation of being a player really doesn't help, nor does the fact that his last relationship has ended just a few months ago and his ex sits right behind him in class while Arnika sits in front.

'Congratulations children,' their English teacher, who is accompanying them, beams. Arnika steps forward and gives her a side hug while Shadab touches her feet.

Arnika notices that and smiles. It's little gestures like these that attract her to him.

Somewhat.

Shadab smiles as he slyly looks upward and catches her looking at him—just the very reason why he's risked spondylitis in the first place.

They begin to walk towards the parking lot to go back to school, in the school car, Innova.

Shadab checks the time.

'12.10 p.m., three periods still to go,' he whispers in Arnika's ear as their teacher increases her stride after she gets a call on her cell phone.

'You want to go back? Can't we just ask ma'am to stop somewhere on the way... I think we need to celebrate!' she exclaims.

'I think we should get back to school... education is important, Arnika Sinha,' he replies very dramatically.

She playfully punches his shoulder.

Another touch in a few minutes; he is loving it today.

They reach the parking lot. Ms Stella, their teacher, is still on the call.

'I can't see the car or the driver anywhere,' Shadab says after scrutinizing the parking lot.

'That guy looked young... he's probably gone to meet his girlfriend or something,' Arnika suggests and they both laugh.

Their teacher returns.

'Where is the driver?' she asks hurriedly. Her facial expressions reflect tension.

'What happened ma'am... Is everything okay?' Arnika enquires.

'I just got a call from my house... my son has fainted... he's not been keeping well,' she ends like a concerned mother.

'So, we can get the driver to drop you first at your place, ma'am,' Shadab suggests.

A car ride to school from their teacher's house with Arnika. Alone. Both of them. Back seats. Comfortable back seats.

Shadab's mind quickly bakes a plan.

'No... my husband is already on his way... he'll pick me from here and we'll go to the hospital directly,' her words work as the perfect icing to his already-baked plan. 'You both go back to school... I'm trying to call the principal ma'am but it's not getting through...'

'We'll inform her,' Shadab quickly suggests.

Arnika gives him a look.

There's something uncanny about his concern for the teacher, she can sense it.

They connect.

'Yes... okay... but where is the driver?' her cell phone rings again and cuts short her question. She walks away from them.

'What's up? Your concern for ma'am... sounds a little unlike you,' is the first observation Arnika makes.

'Come on... her child fainted... poor little thing... having a mother like her is punishing enough,' he plays along well.

Girls get all the more inquisitive when you give confusing answers.

Clear *fundas*. Guaranteed results.

'Ha! Ha?' the annoyance in her voice is evident.

'It's working, it's working,' he says it in his head. Their teacher

returns, cutting their conversation short.

Almost *karmic*, the next minute the school car enters the gate followed by the teacher's husband's car.

'My husband's here,' she says.

'So is the school car,' Shadab replies.

'Okay...children...I expect that you will reach school and behave responsibly...I hope I can trust you two.'

Shadab flashes his perfect put-on innocent smile, complementing it with puppy, liquid eyes.

'Take good care of your son, ma'am,' he says and smiles after she leaves them and goes to talk to the driver before walking to her husband's car.

They both walk to the car and sit inside.

Back seats. Comfortable back seats.

Two minutes later.

'Bhaiya...kya haal hai?' Shadab asks the young driver as Arnika looks on suspiciously.

'Theekh hoon,' he replies.

'*Girlfriend se meeting was good?*' he asks confidently and they both notice the driver blush and avoid the answer.

'Bull's eye,' Shadab whispers into her ear. Arnika smiles back.

'Arnika, aren't you hungry?' his tone is intentionally theatrical and loud.

'Me?...err...a little,' she replies honestly.

He looks at his watch. 12.30 p.m. They still have a good forty minutes.

The debate ended late, there was a lot of traffic on the way and the driver got challaned.

Many reasons. One act. Shadab has thought it all.

'Driver bhaiya also must be so hungry...he's been here since morning...right bhaiya?' he ends softly.

The driver, uneducated but not dumb, understands what the kid is trying to do.

'Bhook toh hai...par madam ne kaha hai ki school he pahuchana hai directly,' the driver slyly says, being well aware that a free lunch is on the cards.

'Yes...but there's so much traffic on the way and ma'am really doesn't have to know...a few minutes here...a few minutes there.'

Arnika smiles as she registers what he's trying to do.

'Hmmm... *raaste mein kuch aae toh... mein bhi kuch kha loon... paanch-dus minute ke liye he,'* the driver says cleverly.

The school is still a few kilometres away. Brick Bakers will come on the way, he quickly analyses.

'So Arnika...coffee?' he smiles.

To bunk is divine, to say no to coffee is sin.

'Sure...but umm...you're confident about this? We are in the school uniform...and I don't have any money on me.'

'Allow me, lady,' he says saucily.

'Okay...but then it'll sound like a date,' she says.

'I don't mind making it look like one too,' he says, raising his hands.

'In your dreams,' she replies in good humour.

'If that's how you want it to be.'

He smiles, she smiles, problem solved.

Brick Bakers.

A single triple-figure ode to Gandhi is all that the driver has taken for the next thirty minutes. And then they say money can't buy time.

They both enter the coffee shop. Most of the tables are occupied by couples. Arnika can smell coffee and love in the air. She has a feeling of knowing what this day might just lead to.

The waiter greets Shadab with warmth reserved for regular customers and leads them to a table, which is not visible from the entrance. Next, he pulls the chair for Arnika.

She simply smiles at this. The guy's social. Got contacts. Got influence.

Once seated, Shadab shoots a faint nod in the waiter's direction and he nods his head in reply, ever more slightly. She's quick to notice though.

'You seem to be a regular here,' she comments, once the waiter leaves.

'Not really…but…yeah…their cold coffee is worth trading life for.'

Cold coffee arrives just a few minutes after he says it. Her coffee has a chocolate-sauce heart, brewing on its top.

'And exactly how many girls have been in the same situation… asked the same question…heard the same answer…seen the same heart?' she asks.

He smiles. She's not an easy nut to crack but he won't stop being the chipmunk too.

'I think none,' he says confidently.

She expected a better answer from him. This is too clichéd.

'Liar,' she accuses him.

'Well honestly, there have been a quite a few but none's been so intelligent to guess all that you have,' he says as he takes a sip from his coffee.

'You're good at this...aren't you?' she brings the straw to her mouth.

'At what? Getting the driver to stop on the way...piece of cake,' he states.

'Even that,' she replies and smiles.

She's smiling too much. He can see it. She can feel it.

A slice of chocolate cake and conversation happen next.

'So...who all in your family?' she asks, taking a bite from the shared slice.

'Mom...Dad...my younger sister...me and loads of money.' He slices off a bite just from where her spoon has attacked the cake.

'Subtle,' she comments.

'Sorry what?' He retorts, obviously trying to ignore the sarcasm.

'Nothing, rich boy.'

He smiles sheepishly. Turns out she's about substance. The type that isn't associated with abuse.

'What about your family?' He quickly tries to change the topic. And to be fair, it's a valid question. Two months, yet they've never really talked in such detail.

'Mine's more about girl power...Mom...me...granny.' Their spoons collide as they attack the same edge of the cake.

Awkward. Not. They both end up smiling. At. With. For. Each other.

'Dad and Mom got separated when I was young,' she suddenly turns pensive.

'I'd love to meet your mother...but that'll be only when you'll invite me home.' His joke has the desired result—the smile's back on her face.

'You won't be able to handle it,' she says vibrantly.

'I'm good with mothers…plus there's an advantage of a no-father clause…this so works for our future,' he winks and smiles.

'You won't try giving up, would you?' she demands.

'Not until you stop smiling.'

He smiles, she smiles, problem solved.

four

That's how he finally asks her out...not before saving her from goons, getting pushed for her in the canteen line, plotting and planning in the game of Truth and Dare, sms'ing her into the night, driving to her house at three in the morning, a red rose and those three words...
I LOVE YOU.

10 July 2009

In school. In class.

Truth and Dare—the game for all seasons, the game played with much reason. The game that every group plays to squeeze out the truth. Correction—embarrassing truth. To open the ancient locks guarding old secrets, to cause disaster. Correction—sweet disaster.

It, perhaps, is the best way to kill a forty-five minute free period when your English teacher is bunking school for a wedding.

The desks have been rearranged to form a circle. Vasu's Nike water tumbler is being spun in the centre. The rules are simple. Questions cannot be passed. Dares cannot be skipped. Truth shall prevail. Bravery shall rule.

Ritesh and Alisha, who are supposed to be in the Commerce section, attending their Business Studies class, are conveniently sitting in the Humanities section with Shadab, Arnika, Vasu, Bani, Saachi and Abhinav.

Convenient coincidence or planned conspiracy, Shadab parks

his firm butt right opposite to where Arnika's firmer butt is parked.

Vasu gets up and spins the bottle with much force. A few rounds of spinning. Anticipation. Who will it be?

It stops. Ritesh is the target.

'Truth or Dare?' the group collectively asks. Talk of sweet slaughter.

'Truth,' Ritesh says confidently.

Everybody darts their questions at him. Most of them unanimously pertain to Alisha and him.

'I will answer only one,' he states plainly. Alisha is visibly embarrassed at the multiples of some large digit number.

'Okay,' Arnika begins. Her voice has a sense of assurity. Vasu, too excited to get his question answered, tries to cut her but Shadab signals him to keep quiet. He complies.

It's the Bro Code.

'So...Ritesh, in this class...apart from Alisha, of course, who's the one girl that turns you on in no time?'

There's a collective hoot. Wicked question. Shadab raises his hand for a Hi5 and she responds.

Positive signs.

Ritesh looks at Alisha. She's expressionless outside; inside all the more anxious to know. He looks at Shadab next. A single second of eye contact. They both know the name he wants to take.

Arnika's hot. Everlasting hot. Namibia's desert-heat hot.

'Rhea,' he finally says.

Alisha. Raised eyebrows. 'I shall remember.'

A balloon of laughter bursts in the group.

Ritesh and Shadab get up together to spin the bottle next, both bending down at the same time.

'Check your mobile...I've sent you a message,' Shadab whispers quickly into his ear before returning to his desk.

The bottle is spun again. Again. Again. It finally stops at Arnika.

'Payback!' Ritesh exclaims. He's gone through Shadab's message in the meantime.

This should be fun.

'Truth,' she says after much deliberation.

'Perfect,' Shadab whispers very softly.

'So... Arnika... what's up between Shadab and you?'

There's a sudden silence. Five pairs of eyes oscillate from Shadab to Arnika. Shadab's eager to know. Arnika too realizes she's been set up. The back of her ears burn.

'Ummm... he's a nice guy.'

'Nice guy,' the boys repeat in unison. Bani nudges Vasu to shut him up while Shadab tries hard to control his smile from bursting into a mad grin. 'And... he's a friend...,' she's finding it hard to choose the correct words.

'Just a friend?' Ritesh, being the guy's best friend, won't let this drop.

'That's more than one question,' Bani complains. The girl's best friend has also come to the rescue.

Shadab's got his answer though.

'Are you blushing, Arnika?' Vasu plots further.

'Huh... no... why would I?'

Inside even she knows it's a lie.

Shadab's smiling.

There's some flow of chemistry for sure.

There's the chance.

There's the likelihood of a LOVE STORY.

♥♥

Of sharing folks and smiles.

11 July 2009

Recess

Shadab, Arnika and Bani are walking towards the school canteen.

Two is company, three is crowd. They've yet not reached the level of walking alone in the school. He wishes for that and how! The little shack which houses probably the most unhygienic food around is abuzz with activity. There's a long queue and the snake-like line slithers as the senior students, much like the SUVs, try to overtake the little Marutis and Santros.

'What's with mothers these days? Nobody gets a tiffin or what?' Bani comments loudly. 'C'mon Shadab…be a man…get in the queue,' she ends.

The girls giggle.

Spotlight.

Chivalry versus hunger.

Impression versus bullying the way to the counter.

Patience versus potato chips.

Thrust versus chilled coke.

'I'll go,' Arnika volunteers.

No. No. No, is all that it echoes in Shadab's head. Hungry guys, well metaphorically and literally and a babe like her in the line. NEVER.

'No…you can't go there,' he says sternly.

'Why?' she's surprised by his assertiveness.

'Because…because,' he's not sure if he should let her know the real reason.

'Because?' she won't let it budge. The feminist in her is aroused.

'Because,' he looks around to find a reason. Luckily, he spots

Rachit, a junior on the debating team, in the first ten students in the queue. 'Rachit's there…Rachit…you need to get something for us too.' He shouts, 'Quick…tell me, what do you guys want to have?'

'Get some coke and noodles,' Bani replies for them. Arnika grabs his hand suddenly, not that he minds but it's sudden for him to get startled.

Her fingers wriggle against his as he looks on, dumbstruck! It just turns out to be Gandhi green.

The brief touch. His hands sticky with sweat. Hers cold. The sensation—electric.

'What's this?' Shadab demands once his body temperature bounces back to equilibrium.

'Money,' she replies in a matter-of-fact tone.

'Dude…come on…I'm not taking this,' he holds her hand and keeps the wrinkled notes back. 'I have a wallet,' he ends, rejoicing in the touch once again.

'Then, I'm not taking anything you get,' Arnika says, determined.

'Arnikaaaa,' he groans in protest.

'What?' she's unfazed. 'You paid for coffee…the other day.'

'You both went for coffee and I don't even know anything about it…Arni…I'm hurt,' Bani, who's been a silent observer to their little fervour, suddenly comes to life with histrionics.

'Shadab bhaiya…what do you need?' the junior shouts from the queue. It's his turn next.

'Shadab bhaiya…bully much?' Arnika asks playfully.

'Respect much,' he says before running towards the junior, leaving the two girls for a minute.

'He didn't want you to get in the line because he feels protective of you,' Bani begins once Shadab has gone.

'Really? Why?' she asks, knowing the answer pretty well.

'It's obvious…he doesn't want any other guy to harm you and

with this figure and face...it's a tough job.'

She blushes and looks at him standing in the queue too, now bearing the Mexican waves rising from behind, just for her.

'By the way...I'm still hurt,' Bani snaps her out of her thoughts.

'Bani...we just went for coffee...after the debate last week.'

'So...was it like a date?' she questions like a prying reporter trying to scoop out sex tips from a menopause-hit celebrity.

'A date...no...I mean...we just...coffee...I mean...no...obviously not...yes...I mean...it can't really be a date...I mean...I don't know,' she's confused. It's not a good sign, she knows it, yet she can't help it.

'Hmmm,' Bani gives a smug smile. 'He really likes you,' she suddenly says.

Arnika prefers to stay quiet. Silence is golden, indeed.

'The way he looks at you...it's so apparent...he's a nice guy too,' she continues, 'and I have a feeling...a tiny little feeling...that's this isn't a one-sided story,' she nudges Arnika.

The blush returns. So does the smile.

'No...I mean...I don't want to get into a relationship...not in 12th...I need a good percentage in my Boards for New York and what will happen once we're over with 12th?' she observes with conviction.

'So you've actually given it a thought?' Bani's quick to grasp and point out. There's a smile on both the girls' faces.

'No...I mean...sometimes...I mean...okay...yes!' she finally confesses it. It feels so good, like a boulder off her chest. Like her food pipe freed from a stuck chicken bone at KFC.

'He's worth it...rich, hot, handsome, even pays all the time...give it a try,' Bani adds quickly as she sees him return, struggling with the coke glasses and the lousy noodles served in the thinnest-possible paper plate.

Arnika rolls her eyes and steps forward to help him out.

'Thank you,' he coughs and adds slowly, 'for supporting me.'

There's an involuntary smile in reaction, on her face. A different smile. A more confusing one for her. A more satisfying one for him.

The flirt's just worked. He knows it. She knows it.

He holds the thin paper plate for them as they dash for the forks. Only two, by the number. Strange, isn't it?

Bani picks up the first in no time.

'Can we share?' he asks her, a little shy.

'We sure can.'

She smiles, he smiles, problem solved.

12 July 2009

7.45 p.m.
'Hello! Hi granny! Sorry, I couldn't take your calls...I was clearing some doubts with sir...yes granny, I know the tuition gets over at seven...no...I haven't reached the parking lot...yes...I'd told the driver to pick me up...no granny...I'm not panting...I'm just climbing down the stairs...oh, you're at Big Bazaar in Shalimar... okay...sorry to keep you waiting...okay granny...let me call the driver now...yes granny...I love you too,' Arnika multitasks by cutting the call, juggling her Economics book and looking for her driver in the market's parking lot where her coaching centre is located.

Bani, Shadab and all her friends and tuition mates had left after the tuition got over at 7 p.m.

A dark evening sky, no known faces around, an old grandmother waiting in the Mall, a city not entirely familiar, a mother who's not in town, a call to the driver which isn't getting through. Arnika feels a punch of confusion and tension hits her stomach.

There's a tinge of uneasiness in her as she stands in the busy market, desperately trying to call her driver.

Just as she is scanning the parking lot in the rectangular market, a car with loud outlandish music, tinted glasses, neon lights and some boys, speeds past her, almost within a millimetre of her.

'Assholes,' she shouts and shows them the finger. The car screeches to a halt immediately and the driver reverses the car to where she's standing.

'Oops,' she mutters as soon as she sees the car getting reversed.

Unknown city.

Unknown guys in a group.

Definitely not good.

She contemplates on calling the cops. Bad idea. She desperately calls her driver again. Same response. Not reachable.

The sky suddenly turns a shade darker.

The driver, a young boy with piercings, gelled hair and all that jazz, rolls down the windows and the boy sitting on the passenger seat, a lookalike friend of the driver, grins and questions, 'You said something?'

Arnika ignores the question and tries calling her driver again. Still not reachable.

The guy starts to laugh loudly.

'Economics...nice...what's the price level?' the one sitting behind questions and more laughter rebounds off their car.

Though bold, she feels tears swell up in her eyes. The guys continue to sneer at her.

Arnika turns around to go back to the tuition. Just as she's ready to take another step, she hears a loud screech of car tyres and turns around, only to find the boys' car surrounded by two cars and a familiar back frame bending over the passenger's door. Low-waist jeans. Muscular body. Spiked hair.

'Shadab,' she whispers with joy.

Telepathy or he's actually heard her whisper his name, he turns around the same moment and signals her to come to him.

Confused, she walks up to him.

'Arnika...my friends here have something to say to you,' he says politely. She tries not to look at the boys in the car.

'Sorry,' the boy on the passenger seat mutters.

'Better,' Shadab pats his shoulder through the open window and signals Arnika to go and sit in his car which is just parked behind the boys' car.

Once he makes sure she's seated inside safely, he turns back to them. 'Next time...you try doing this to anybody...just remember...now quickly get the hell out of here.'

Arnika witnesses the boys reverse their car by a few inches and speed away in a jiffy. She smiles as Bani's words in the canteen haunt her.

'He's protective of you.'

She sees Shadab walk up to the car standing in front of the boys' car and have a friendly word with the burly old guys sitting in it.

'Thank you boss,' Shadab shakes one of the burly guy's hand. 'They know who Billa bhaiya is,' he continues.

The burly guy smiles back.

'Don't worry, Shadab...okay, now go...she's waiting in the car.' There's a mild laugh from the muscular friends and he walks back to his car.

She's on a call with her granny when he opens the door and sits inside.

'Yes...granny...I've also been trying his number for a long time...I know he's an idiot...no no...don't call for a cab...I'm coming to pick you up...,' she looks at Shadab as he brings the car into ignition. 'I luckily met one of my friends in the market...I'm coming with him...yes granny...he's a very nice boy,' she pauses and whispers into her cell phone, 'no, he's not my boyfriend.'

He smiles at this and moves the car into first gear.

'Okay, now stop embarrassing me...,' she covers her face with her hand and looks away from him. 'I'm coming. Bye.'

'Shadab, I don't know how to thank you enough,' she begins as soon as the call is cut.

'From where do we pick your grandmother?' he asks mechanically.

'Oh...Shalimar Mall,' she ends confused and starts looking down at her feet.

'If the guys were troubling you...you could have called me on your own...I thought we were friends,' his voice has a subtle tone of hurt.

'I know...I'm sorry...but I got so confused...the driver's cell was unreachable...Mom's not in town...granny's waiting for me at the Mall for such a long time...I couldn't see anyone known around...I got so scared,' she ends softly only to escalate her tone with a sudden clap, 'by the way...how did you come to know?... And who were those guys you shook hands with in the car, which was standing in front and...and...what exactly did you say to the jerks in the other car?' she darts the questions at breath-taking speed.

'Breathe first,' he says, stopping at a red light. 'Billa bhaiya... local *Sarkar Raj*...,' he gauges the confused expression on her face and continues, 'it's a guy thing...you need to have contacts with all types of people...for situations like these...don't go too deep into it.'

The signal turns green and he accelerates the car with a heavy push on the accelerator pedal.

'Careful,' she warns him.

'Your grandmother must be tired...we need to hurry,' he says, speeding the car and honking to make way.

She feels a blush creep on to her cheeks. Something's happening to her.

His concern. Her grandmother.

'But you still didn't tell me how you reached there all of a sudden?' she asks to kill the awkward moment.

'I was standing at the juice corner at the rear end with Billa bhaiya and his friends and when the car reversed...one of his friends commented on how a sexy girl was getting harassed,' he replies, swiftly overtaking the car in front.

'Right,' she smiles uncomfortably.

He looks at her. 'C'mon...be okay with it...people do think you're sexy,' he says with a twinkle in his eye. Flirt king.

'But why were you at the juice corner...the class ended at seven...I thought you must have gone home.'

'I was,' he pauses, 'waiting for you.' He ends softly.

There are those certain moonlight moments where silence does the talking. They both experience the same at this point of time.

She fakes a cough to change the scenario. 'And the jerks?... You actually made them apologize to me.'

'I would have smashed their balls...had I not promised Mom, I won't fight,' he points towards a cut on his eyebrow. '13 stitches... bad fight...gang war...outside school.'

'Why?' she interjects.

'Rhea...same story,' he says hesitantly.

'Your ex? Right?'

'Yes,' he says, looking ahead at the road.

'Ummm...if you don't mind my asking...'

'We wanted different things...it wasn't her fault...I think it was me...anyway, drop that.'

There's a silence in the car for the next few minutes.

'That's the Mall,' Arnika finally says as she sees the glass building. She calls her grandmother and enquires about her whereabouts. 'She's sitting at the entrance of Big Bazaar...Gate Number 4...I think we'll have to park the car and walk till there.'

'No worries,' he turns into the employees' driveway and drives the car till the security checkpoint.

'What are you doing?' she questions, confused, as the security guard whistles, asking them to stop.

He chooses to stay silent till the guard approaches them.

'Sir...this driveway is only for the employees,' the security guard says in a done-to-death officer tone.

'You're telling me...what's your name? Rampal,' he reads from the guard's name plate and pretends to dial in some numbers on his cell. 'Just because this car doesn't have a sticker...he thinks he'll stop me...the son of the owner of Big Bazaar,' he says with such arrogance that even the guard is perplexed. Arnika tries hard not to grin.

The security guard goes back to the security room to have a word with his equally gullible colleague. They both come back to the car. 'Yes sir?' the new guy asks politely.

'Raise the damn roadblock pole...who do you want to talk to...the manager of Big Bazaar...or the manager of your security company. He's a theatre artist. He can't go wrong with this. The guards retire to a corner, discuss only to finally raise the pole and let the car pass without any checking either.

'That was neat,' Arnika comments, once they've crossed the guards.

'And they say public places in India are safe,' he laughs as he halts the car right outside Gate Number 4. She gets out of the car and runs towards Big Bazaar.

Five minutes later, Shadab sees her support a smart, old woman with freckles and a posh white bun, wearing jeans and a top, walk towards the car. They are followed by two huge trolleys full of grocery being pushed by the store workers.

He quickly runs his hand through his hair, gets down and opens the boot of the car. 'Get them here,' he instructs the workers as they struggle with the heavy trolleys.

'Granny, this is Shadab,' Arnika introduces him.

Shadab bends down and touches her feet. Arnika notices that again. Respect. She's liking all of this.

'Thank you beta…we've caused you enough trouble,' her grandmother says softly. Shadab smiles back, silently admiring the glacier who's passed clear genetic water to the current stream.

'Come…aunty…sit,' he opens the car door for her and helps her sit, giving her his shoulder for support and brushing against Arnika's arm slightly. He closes the door gently and they both walk back to the boot where the workers have loaded the grocery. He tips the workers, thanks them and walks over to open Arnika's door.

'You know what Shadab?' she begins as he opens the passenger door, 'you're a nice guy and I'm glad we are friends.'

'Just friends?' he fakes a grimace and smiles.

'At least for now,' she closes the door and smiles.

Problem solved.

That night… love finds a way in SpongeBob boxers.

12.30 a.m.
That single message in your inbox. That notification. That Facebook status. That mention of your name in her post. That special person posting something on your wall.

It just makes your day or in Shadab's case, your night.

'So the next time I'm in a sticky situation, I know whom to call… Shadab Parvez,' is what Shadab sees as Arnika's status, once he logs in to his Facebook, after having dinner. A few likes, a few comments, have already made their presence felt.

So the entire school will have something to discuss tomorrow.

He pings her on the BBM messenger. Communication comes cheap with the coloured berry.

So, I think you should have my number on speed dial now :P:P

He finally types the first message after much deliberation. The first message is the most important—a careful use of words and emoticons paves the way for the hundreds to follow.

Three minutes. One hundred eighty seconds. A roller coaster of emotions and thoughts later, his cell screen blinks. He tosses around in his bed and excitedly reads the reply.

Ha ha! Does that mean, you want me to fall in trouble all the time :O
PS—My grandmother thinks there's something going on between us… ha ha ha!

He jumps on his bed and gets up. He reaches for the cordless and dials Ritesh's number.

'Get Alisha in the conference and don't ask any questions,' the first thing he says in a hurried tone as soon as the call is answered.

'Okayyyy,' Ritesh yawns and dials Alisha's number and connects her in the conference.

Alisha: *Hi Marshmallow! Missing me?*
Ritesh: *Errr... Alisha.*
Shadab: *Ha ha ha... she calls you Marshmallow... ha ha ha... Alisha... ha ha ha ha!*
Alisha: *Oh... hi Parvez.*
Ritesh: *Yes... it's a conference call... anyway... Shadab... why'd you wake us up?*
Alisha: *I wasn't sleeping.*
Ritesh: *But you told me you're going to sleep... some time back.*
Alisha: *Yeah... but then, I didn't feel like sleeping.*
Ritesh: *Then you should have called me.*
Shadab: *Oi... you both... I HAVE A PROBLEM HERE!!!*
Ritesh: *Yeah... say.*
Alisha: *Yes.*
Shadab: *Okay... so I was just chatting with Arnika on BBM...*
Ritesh and Alisha: *Not again!!!! Shadab, all we've heard since evening is Arnika... stop man.*
Shadab: *Fuck you both... selfish people... anyway... listen... so I was talking to her and she messages me... my grandmother thinks we are going out... what's your take... that's positive, right? AND... ANSWER SOON... IT'S BEEN MORE THAN FIVE MINUTES... I NEED TO REPLY ASAP.*
Ritesh: *I think... I think... I think... I need sleep.*
Shadab: *FUCK YOU!*
Alisha: *Chill Parvez... just play along... stop acting so gay.*
Ritesh: *Dude... she's a girl... a goddamn girl... we're programmed to master them.*

Alisha: *Hmmm… for the sake of our three-year old relationship, I'll pretend I did not hear that Ritesh.*
Shadab: *Can you both stop? I need a reply before the next leap year.*
Alisha: *Okay… breathe… now type what I say.*
Shadab: *Okay… say.*
Alisha: *Isn't it strange how your grandmother and I think alike… and send the subtle smile emoticon along?*
Shadab: *Done.*
Ritesh: *Now can we sleep? I need to get up for football practice.*
Shadab: *Get lost… Alisha, I'll call you directly.*
Ritesh: *Hmmm… I think I can stay up for a while.*
Alisha: *Ha ha ha… insecure much… Ritu!*
Ritesh: *Don't EVER call me Ritu.*
Alisha: *Okay, Ritu.*
Shadab: *Guys… she replied.*
Ritesh: *And I farted.*
Alisha: *Ignore him Shadab… what does she say?*
Shadab: *Okay… I'll read out the entire message… did you just sleep by any chance? Anyway, my grandmother also thinks that this time is not for falling in love… it's time for education.*
Ritesh: *HA HA HA HA… dude… she's killer.*
Alisha: *Oh! She just owned you.*
Shadab: *What do I say now? Why is she so good at this?*
Ritesh: *I vote we all should sleep… all in favour… say Ritesh, you're a rockstar.*
Alisha: *I'll call you Shadab… go to sleep, Ritu.*
Ritesh: *Don't call me Ritu!!*
Shadab: *You know what? You both… seriously… go get a life… and before that… get a room.*

He cuts the call and falls back on to his bed.

'So how do you manage this?' he types in next.

'Manage what?' she replies back almost instantly.

'Kill every move I make,' he knows it's a gamble but he increases the stake and types next.

'Ha ha...what happened to the player?' her next message reads.

She thinks he's a player. Negative. Very negative.

He punches his pillow in desperation. There's something his brain needs to come up with. It always has to. With Ruchi, Sneha, Kruti, Urvika and Rhea.

'The player's taken a lifetime retirement...t&c apply*.'

He's already imagining the smile on her face as he sends the message. He knows he's typed a perfect rebound.

One minute. Two painful minutes. Three very painful minutes. Five intolerable minutes. Ten excruciating minutes pass. No reply.

Sending another message or calling would risk him being portrayed as someone desperate and cheap. Much like the others she's rejected.

Add twenty more minutes. A hundred tosses and turns in the bed. A thousand times of unlocking the cell and searching the screen unsuccessfully for a reply.

Imagine a natural, naked guy hanging in mid-air by a rope, oscillating between a swimming pool full of blondes in bikinis and on the other side are babes giving lap dances and lots of free beer. He'd feel the heat, the passion. Yet, he'll be hopeless. Restless. That's exactly what Shadab feels.

Suddenly, there's a flash of lightning in his head and he jumps out of his bed, throws his T-shirt over him, slips his feet into his slippers, sprays some deo, pops in some gum, glides his hand repeatedly through his hair as he carefully opens the door to his room, stealthily crosses his parents' room, picks up the keys to his car and like every other sneak, tips the night guard, then sits in his car, frees the handbrake, presses the clutch of his Endeavour, pulls the gear into neutral and gets the guard to push down the car from the driveway on to the road and quickly drives away, first to 24x7 florist and then…

'Uh…hello.'

Arnika looks at the name flashing on her mobile screen and answers the call, after a few rings. It's 2.15 a.m.

'Listen…firstly, I'm sorry to wake you up…I know I shouldn't have called you at this time but I had to…I mean I didn't want to but…I mean…,' Shadab begins in an apologetic tone.

'Shadab…breathe…I wasn't even sleeping,' she cuts him and says coolly.

'Oh,' is all that comes in reply from him.

'Ummm…so?' she asks a little apprehensively.

'So…so…where are you?' he feels his throat turn dry.

'As queer as it may sound, but I'm generally home at what,' she checks the time, '2.45 a.m., on a school night especially.' She pauses briefly and asks, 'Are you okay?'

'Me…yes…never…been…butter…I mean better,' his tongue slips, heartbeat skips.

'You sure?…Not been doing pot?' she jokingly asks.

'No baba…not six hours before school,' he tries hard to sound normal.

'What's that noise behind you? You're in a car?' she enquires next.

'Yes…how did you guess?' he shoots back instantly.

'The sound of the engine…hey wait…this sound,' she gets up from her bed and walks up to the window of her room and draws the curtain. 'YOU'RE OUTSIDE!' her voice rises and dies much like the Sensex, as she realizes her grandmother's sleeping in the adjoining room.

'Err…yes…Actually I was just passing by, so I thought…I'd stop and say Hi!' he says softly.

'Hi, at 2.45 a.m.?'

'Listen…I know this might sound very strange and inappropriate…but can you come out for five minutes?' he almost whispers.

'No,' she says simply.

'Please…it's very urgent…I won't be able to sleep otherwise and I mean it,' the plead in his voice is at its strongest.

Arnika has an idea of what's going to happen next. It's the same reason for which she had not replied to his message, some time back.

Yet, a part of her, beating way too heavily for a normal telephonic conversation, argues over her rational mind and signals her to say, 'Okay…five minutes maximum.'

The mirror is generally not her comrade, yet today, after deliberating and finally deciding to not change her clothes and go out in her night pyjamas and T-shirt, she switches on the light of her room and spends a good two minutes before it. Setting her hair. Letting the strands fall over her eyes. She read somewhere that it romanticizes the situation.

She closes the door of her room softly and walks over to her granny's room to press her ear over the door.

Snoring. Sweet music.

She very quietly walks over to the main door, opens it. After ensuring no neighbour is outside, she opens the side gate of her house with much patience and technique, before coming out and walking a confident and casual walk to his car.

He's wondering how often she has done this, as he sees her walk with a certain air of confidence and assurity to his car. He opens the passenger door, while seated, for her and she smiles. Without reason. With emotion.

He accelerates the car slowly and stops it a little ahead of her house, under a huge *peepal* tree. With cover enough to let nobody spot them. Not even the stray dogs who are policing the roads as masters of the night.

Striated moonlight peeps in through the windshield as he looks at her.

Soft music. His favourite CD in the background.

She's looking down.

He's pursing his lips repeatedly.

'Those...are...nice boxers...SpongeBob,' she says suddenly and they both burst out laughing. Talk of killing the moonlight moment.

'Thank you,' he says, a little embarrassed. The realization that she's seen his almost bare hairy legs sends a current in his body and the result is well...a little hormonal, for such a deep situation.

'Arnika,' he pauses briefly, 'there's something which I've kept hidden from you all this time...and...I need your advice on it,' he says, placing his hand over his thighs. Very strategically.

'What?' she asks confused and quickly looks towards her house again.

Sneak outs aren't her diet for the night.

'There's this girl you also know,' he shifts in his seat and continues hesitantly, 'who, I think, I've fallen for...and I'm scared if I should tell her or not...because her friendship is as important to me as probably teddy bears are to girls.'

'Oh!' a flurry of emotions rise inside her. A dog howls in the distance and she looks away to fight back a strange sensation which is assaulting her heart.

She's read *Mills & Boons* where the guy always confesses his feelings for the girl to his best friend. Is she just a friend for him?

'Arnika...Arnika,' he repeats her name softly to break her trance.

'YES...,' she blinks hard.

'So...what do you think?' he asks.

'I think you should let her know,' she says half-heartedly. There's a slight hope that the name in his heart and soon to be on those silky lips is the same as the image which bounces off the mirror of his car.

'You sure?' he asks again.

'Yes,' she replies and adds, 'was this all you wanted to ask... seriously? I've risked it for something so...trivial.' There's a tinge of irritation in her voice.

He fights the Mount Everest urge to not to smile back.

'Yes...so, do you want to go for a drive? Some coffee maybe?' he asks, changing the topic.

'No,' she opens the car door and quickly steps out and turns around, 'I better get going...coming out so late in the night...this isn't exactly me.'

He gives a mild laugh and thanks her and says, 'I'm going to tell her then.'

'Cool,' she turns around and starts to walk to the main gate of her house. Her cell beeps in the quiet night as she opens the gate and she freezes, wondering if it's her grandmother. She slowly reaches for her cell, not even looking back, if he's left or not.

This is what tension does to you. Piss pressure.

She reads the message. It's from him.

Turn around.

She turns around, wondering if all of this is a joke but her apprehension metamorphoses into a blush as soon as she sees him bending on one knee with a rose in his hand.

There are those quiet unavoidable moments. The lull before the storm. The calm before the first wax. The silence when an underage girl goes in for a pregnancy test.

He's looking at her expectantly. She's transfixed as if her nervous system has gone into a coma.

'Okay... I shouldn't be saying this... but my knees hurt,' he says, trying not to be loud.

They both burst out laughing.

Sweet laughter. Different laughter.
A laugh indicating the good days to come.

five

So what do you discuss on your first dinner date?
Your exs and their kissing capabilities, the waiter's sexy butt,
what happens in a ladies room? Well…that's how it goes…

27 July 2009

Mainland China. Chinese. Expensive Chinese. Her favourite. He's found out. Her Facebook profile. Social networking does help.

8.45 p.m. That's what the dial of his Dad's Tissot indicates as he waits outside the restaurant in a crisp black formal shirt and faded denims. He's begged for the watch from him.

Tonight is special. Very special.

Arnika's finally agreed for a dinner date. Their first dinner date.

For her mother, she's going for dinner with Alisha and her cousins, who've come from Canada. Lying isn't her thing but she wants to be sure about him, about them, before she can let her mother know. The past hasn't been so kind. It's a classic case of once bitten twice shy.

Alisha's car stops right outside the restaurant after ten minutes. Ritesh is driving it. Alisha is sitting parallel to him while her cousins are sitting on the back seats.

He peeps in the car to find Arnika.

'How about a "Hi" first?' Alisha verbally pokes into his ribs and laughter rebounds the car.

'We'll pick her up by 10.30 p.m.,' Ritesh begins and Alisha adds,

'please remember, it's a public place and PDA is so totally uncool.'
There's more laughter as Arnika gets out of the car.

Body-hugging one piece. Off shoulder. Till the knees. It blows him off his feet.

'Hi!' she says, pulling back the hair strands behind her ear, after they've left.

'You look beautiful,' he gasps. Time stops. It literally does for him.

She smiles in response, bringing her hand to his chin and giving it a slight upward push to close his dropped jaw.

'I'm sss…sorry,' he mutters embarrassed and raises his arm to escort her like a gentleman. 'Shall we?' he asks, not being able to meet her eye.

She encircles her hand around his arm, avoiding his eyes and they both walk hand in hand inside the restaurant, literally looking in opposite directions.

The hostess guides them to the table he's already got reserved.

Inside the Gazebo.

Away from public glare.

With candles and expensive signature cutlery.

It'll cost him enough for two weeks of eating at home and asking Ritesh to drive him around. Petrol comes expensive. Even for love.

They get seated.

'Bottled water,' he says softly to the waiter.

'Why? We are okay with the regular water,' she pauses from replying to her mother's text and says with conviction.

He's taken aback. She's the first girl who's actually been so economically thoughtful. It's a century. Literally saved.

'Okay...normal water should be good.'

The waiter suppresses a frown and leaves only to return after two silent minutes with the jug and menu cards.

He hands the drinks menu to Shadab and the food menu to Arnika. Just like any other couple.

She takes a careful sip from the glass and looks at the menu card. He scans the drinks menu, debating if he should order beer or coke. Neat impressions. Pun intended.

'What do you want to have?' They both question each other at the same time.

And start laughing awkwardly. The waiter throws up internally at the exuberance of puppy love.

'You say,' she says.

'No, you say,' he retorts.

'Okay...starters?' she asks.

'Anything you say,' he replies back.

'How about spinach soup then?' she says with a straight face while his stomach churns in the negative at the very sound of the name. He forces a smile as she asks the waiter to get two, looking at him through the corner of her eye.

'And chicken dimsums and chocolate spring rolls,' she adds. He relaxes a little. Normal food.

'And what would you like to drink along with it?' the waiter asks next.

'Hard or soft?' Shadab tilts his head, asking her naughtily.

She rolls her eyes, indicating the presence of the waiter, as they both smirk. 'Sick,' she says without volume to her voice.

'A diet coke for me,' he says.

'And a Heineken light,' she adds.

Both the guys look at her. The waiter. The boyfriend.

She simply smiles as the waiter leaves.

'So...how's aunty?' he says, spreading the napkin on his thighs. Well mannered. She makes a mental note.

'She's fine...this UN work is driving her crazy and she's driving me crazy,' she smiles.

'And when do I get to be with the crazy girls together?' He regrets what he's said even before he's finished the sentence.

Awkward silence.

'I...I meant...,' he begins apologetically only to be cut short by her laughter.

Understanding. He makes a mental note.

'Soon...very soon...I'm not sure you'll be able to handle her though,' she says next.

The waiter brings in the drinks. He offers the bottle to Arnika to get the temperature checked but she signals him to get it done from Shadab. An instantaneous smile lights up his face.

Importance. Mental note made once again.

Arnika asks the waiter to get the soup first.

'So...Arnika...why won't I be able to handle your mother?'

'Because...she's...,' she pauses, 'you'll know,' she ends as the waiter returns with the soup.

He serves the soup. Posh-hospital quality. Spinach. Hospital. Full power.

She steals a quick look at him to gauge his expression. Stoic. Sick.

She takes a sip from the soup and exclaims, 'Yummm!'

He mirrors the act, only that his 'yummm' sounds more like he's being threatened to castration if he says otherwise.

'You know what Shadab?' she asks, turning serious.

'Yes,' he cringes as the soup enters his food pipe.

'You don't need to do this.'

'Do?' he coughs. 'What?'

'Have this sewage-coloured soup just because I like it.'

He stops midway through his soup. 'I...I,' he's at a loss for words.

Arnika is different. Period. He concludes.

'I mean,' she reaches for his hand and presses it. 'I don't want you to change yourself for me...having diet coke won't impress me when we both know you want a beer too...'

He smiles sheepishly, like when the mother takes her little boy to the ladies room, in the absence of the father and the little boy has no other option.

'Moreover, let's get certain things straight first.' Her eyes contract. They always do, when she means butt-kick business. 'This relationship...there needs to be a limit...what I feel for you is special...but...I don't want this to become a burden.'

He feels a bad taste overpower his mouth. It's not the soup. He's listening or rather digesting everything with patience and pinches of salt. Large globules of salt.

'What I feel for you...I've never felt this way before,' she continues. He smiles.

'But...' she pauses again. The smile dies again.

'I don't want this to affect our studies...our career plans... New York...or your college,' she ends and signals the waiter to open the beer.

She needs a large sip. He needs a dozen. Heavy talk.

'Can...I...get one too...quick,' he asks the waiter as he opens the beer for her. Two minutes and beer is served to him. He takes a large sip.

The beer hits his stomach and his voice rises. Buoyancy.

'I know what you mean...It's just that...I don't want to lose you,' he says and presses her hand softly.

'You won't...all I meant to say was...we need to give this relationship a try but...worst scenario...if we fall out of love... we would still be cordial,' she places her hand over his.

'We won't...I've always been a good boyfriend,' he says.

'Always?' she raises her eyebrows. 'For how many?' she asks, taking another sip.

The soup lies neglected.

'Okay...let's see,' he pretends to scratch his chin. 'Can't remember,' he winks.

'It's easier for me,' she hits back. 'Rahul...Vikram...Ajit.' Hits back hard.

He takes another sip from the beer can.

'And...I'm just kidding...it's just Vikram and you know about it,' she says.

'And you know about Rhea,' he says in his defence.

'Not entirely...the best I know is the looks she's been giving me since the last one month.'

'Rheaaa,' he takes a deep breath, 'those lips...God I miss them,' he exclaims, just to check how possessive she feels.

'I know what you mean,' she's says very coolly, to his surprise. 'Vikram was such a tongue teaser,' she ends, giving a dreamy look.

'Oi!' his effort backfires.

'Yeah?' she replies unaffected.

He smiles. She's just what he's been looking for in every girl. Coffee. Low sugar. Addictive.

'You're looking very pretty today,' he says, changing the topic.

'Does that turn you on?' It's her turn to get naughty.

'The washroom's just down the aisle...I've always wondered what's it like inside the ladies room...except the private cabins...,' he reaches the zenith of his naughtiness and she throws her napkin at him.

'Hey!' he dodges the napkin and the middle-aged couple sitting in the adjacent table smiles at them. Memories of fresh love. Later on. Just memories.

They are talking animatedly when a new, young waiter comes in to take the order for the main course.

Arnika graces the waiter with a proper checkout as Shadab scans the menu card, yet the corner of his eyes are receptive enough to see what's happening.

'Liked his butt?' Shadab asks after he sees Arnika stare at the waiter as he walks away.

'Hmm...it's firm...what's your take?' she says, inching a little forward to get an angled view.

'You do realize it's your boyfriend you're talking to,' he says in a matter-of-fact tone.

'Yes,' she winks at him.

'You know what? Your thought process...it's not like the girls I've been with.'

'Your loss...if you expect me to be this Fevicol-promoting girlfriend who literally sits on your chest all the time...it's still easy...you can leave...I'll pay.'

'Why should I? I can two-time you easily that way.'

'Na...I can't think of kissing already-kissed lips.'

'So does that imply you want to kiss me?'

'You know what? Had you stuck to diet coke, things would have been different...I don't want our first kiss to be so smelly... so,' she gets up suddenly, bends over the table and plants a quick peck on his cheek.

Silence. They both are stunned. The level of frankness. Unbelievable!

'Thank you,' he finally mutters and her cell phone rings in the next instant.

'Mom,' she murmurs and gets up.

Great timing. Indian mothers. They have inbuilt radars which blink every time their girl is doing something they believe she shouldn't. Cell phones create the rest of the problem.

She returns after a few minutes. Food has arrived in the meantime. Prawns, fried rice, American chop suey and schezwan chicken.

'All good?' he asks.

'Yes…,' she says, sitting down. 'I think I should tell her…the whole lying thing…it's too much of a task,' she says, serving him some fried rice.

'Ummm…that'll be all,' he touches her hand softly to stop her from serving more.

The touch. The gaze collision. Electric. Even after a month.

She quickly retreats her hand. It's the first time she's felt the sensation too.

Chemicals and hormones are secreted. Love is pure chemistry.

She signals for the waiter and on his arrival asks him to serve the rest.

She's quiet. Unknown feelings do that to you. He's reciprocating the silence. The difference. He knows what he feels.

'Arnika.'

'Yyes,' she's replies, concentrating on the little shrimp on her plate.

'I love you.' It's just a whisper from him, yet it means a lot to her.

Suddenly.

Shouts don't matter.

Words don't matter.

It's the emotions they feel.

It's probably love!

six

The first time they kiss…sparks fly…it gets smoky, well literally.

2 August 2009

There's an unnatural bounce in Shadab's steps, a rare whistle on his lips as he opens the main door to his house and walks straight to his mother's room, throwing the school bag on the way.

Some four hours earlier.

Economics class

Chit passing between Shadab and Arnika

> Arnika: *I feel like having a chocolate brownie with hazel nuts and lots of chocolate sauce.*

The teacher turns her face towards the blackboard and Arnika quickly throws the chit to Shadab, who is seated right in front of her.

> Shadab: *I know how to bake chocolate brownies. Delicious brownies.*

The teacher is facing the class now, Shadab accidentally drops his pen on the floor and bends down to pick it, not before coughing mildly to inform her of the position of the chit. The next second, her pen also falls down, accidentally of course, and she bends down to pick it.

Strange, very strange!

She tears the last page from her register and writes a new chit.

Arnika: *You do!!!! Wow! I think my Mom's really going to like you then... the last time I tried baking a cake for her, it turned out to be the oven's last day.*

Their teacher continues to blab something about scarcity while Arnika inconspicuously keeps the chit, from behind, in the gap between Shadab's neck and shirt collar.

Shadab senses the touch and pretends to scratch his neck and picks up the chit, reads it, smiles and replies.

Shadab: *I could teach you. Why don't you come over today evening? You could meet Mom too, she's been pestering me to get her to meet you.*

He turns around and places the chit on her desk. He's just asking for a pen, for the records.

Arnika: *You told her about us?*

And she taps him and slides forward the next chit.

Shadab: *Yup... actually she came to know herself. I think my smile is a giveaway.*

The chit passing continues...

Arnika: *Oh! I haven't really told Mom. I know! Next week, it's her birthday. You can help me organize a surprise party for her. We'll call the rest of the gang too and then I'll introduce you to Mom.*

And it still continues.

Shadab: *Great... we'd bake them together... lots of chocolate... a little sugar... spiced with some sauce.*

And another chit is passed.

Arnika: *YOU ARE SICK.*

Can they stop now?

Shadab: *And you love me for that.*

I've given up the count of chits exchanged.

Arnika: *I don't love you.*
Shadab: *Okay... 5 p.m. sounds good.*
Arnika: *When did I say I'm coming?*
Shadab: *Great! 5 p.m. it is then.*

Just as Shadab is about to give her the chit, another chit is launched into Arnika's direction from the adjacent row.

Bani: *Arnika... stop having chit sex with him!*
Arnika: *Ha ha! But I was just on the verge of it. Can I complete, please Bani? Ha ha ha!*
Arnika: *Fine, five it is then. Shadab... about your Mom... any information that'll help.*
Shadab: *Hmmm... let's see now... I think... all you need to do is to be yourself.*
Arnika: *And your Dad, will he be home too?*
Shadab: *Na... he's touring... Mom's going to be in a good mood.*
Arnika: *And your younger sister?*
Shadab: *And Bhittal bhaiya, Neera didi and the drivers and*

the gardener... seriously Arni...
Arnika: *Idiot.*
Bani: *Ha ha... no, you cannot.*

'So, Ms. Bani here, would be kind enough to share, whatever important piece of information she is noting down on that little piece of paper?' Their teacher catches Bani writing the chit.

Arnika: *OH, SHIT.*
Shadab: *Copy that.*

The bell for recess rings suddenly and everybody gets up quickly, giving ample time to Bani to tear the chit. Phew. All hail the empty stomachs.

'Mom!!!' Shadab shouts as he opens the door to his mother's room. She's sitting on the bed, watching her favourite soap.

Wrong timing. Mothers don't like getting disturbed, especially when their favourite soap is airing. That the soap has the same storyline as every other and it hardly requires concentration is a different story.

Yet, breaching the 'mother and serial' code, his mother switches off the television set and exclaims with surprise. It's not often that her son walks straight into her room, after school.

'Is it my birthday... or have you forgotten the way to your room?'

'Very funny, Ma... you know I love you,' he says, kicking off his school shoes and jumping on to the bed. A side hug follows.

'Now seriously, Shadab... what is it? Money... a complaint from school, again? I'm calling your father... this is the limit,' she reaches for her cell phone.

'Mom...no...there's no complaint,' he takes the phone from her hand and disconnects the call. 'Guess who's coming home today evening?' His eyebrows bounce with anticipation.

'Arnika,' she says in the next second.

'Wow...how'd you guess?' he asks.

'Because I'm your mother,' she simply says and smiles. He ruffles his hair in embarrassment.

'Okay...so we are going to bake brownies,' he begins sceptically and adds confidently, 'just for you...so could you ask Bhittal bhaiya to get everything arranged in the kitchen?'

'Brownies...I wish my husband was that caring...'

He begins before she can end, 'But he helped you to get me and Mehreen.'

She laughs heartily, 'And my kitchen?'

Mothers are touchy about kitchens. It's like their place of pilgrimage.

'We won't make any mess...I swear.'

'Okay...now go change your clothes and come down for lunch,' his mother says quickly before switching on the TV as he gets up from the bed and walks towards the door. 'Wait,' she says suddenly and he stops and turns around. 'What about the Economics test? Weren't you supposed to get the results today?'

Memory and mothers. Why?

'Oh that...I got it,' he turns around again, to go to his room.

'Where do you think you're going, mister? What's your score?' she asks, switching off the TV again.

This won't be good.

'Mom...it's just a class test...I mean...'

'Score?' she simply asks.

'Fourteen,' his vocals lose all courage as he murmurs.

'FOURTEEN?' The next time the word is repeated, it bounces off the walls of the room.

'But the highest score was nineteen,' he tries to reason.

'And who is that? Richa?' she asks, her hands on the keypad of her cell phone again.

'No...Richa's got an eighteen...Arnika creamed her.' There's a sudden pride in his voice.

'Then what's she doing with you? Oh, is it like she's the one to control you...overpower you...Okay?' His mother knows what strings to pull. After all, her son is another species of the class called Men. An EGO BASH is just what is needed here.

Shadab ignores her and closes the door with a bang, not without making a mental note of scoring on par with Arnika in the next test that they take.

That evening...

A liberal dose of soap. Some layers of shower gel. Loofah. Pumice stone. Shampoo. Conditioner. Strawberry-flavoured toothpaste. Then Listerine. Everything that can be smuggled from his sister's washroom has been duly smuggled. He needs to look hi-fi. Chiselled. Saucy. Smooth. Sexy as gay.

He finishes the rendezvous with the water queen in the washroom, wraps a towel and walks out to his room. He quickly scans his cupboard. Tommy boxers. A&F shorts. CK slippers. An extra-long, extra-loose Tommy Hilfiger T-shirt.

He's fixing his hair when there's a loud bang at his room's door.

'Who is it?' he asks as he holds the key in the lock of his door.

'WHERE IS MY CONDITIONER?' Mehreen, his fifteen-year-old sister shouts from the other side.

'Err...I...I...I don't have it,' he says timidly, not opening the door.

She kicks on the door again.

'I know you have it Shadab...Bhittal bhaiya saw you take it from my washroom...open the door...I'm getting late for my Salsa class,' she screams again.

Typical brother-sister relationship. A little sugar. A lot of spice.

'Okay...chill...I'll get it,' he says as he turns around and walks to the washroom, glancing at the clock on the way. 5.10 p.m. 'She should be here any moment now,' he mutters as he walks back to the door, holding the conditioner in hand.

There's another knock on the door.

'CAN'T YOU WAIT?' he shouts angrily. 'Here,' he opens the room's door.

'Hi Shadab!' the voice is familiar. Too familiar.

'Arr...ni...ka,' he gulps in panic and looks around. Mehreen has left. 'Hhi...,' he utters after a detailed pause. 'Sorry...I mean...I thought it was my sister,' he tries to clarify.

'Yes...I met her on the way...what's that in your hand?' she looks at the conditioner. Mango flavour.

'Oh...that,' he tries to hide the conditioner and play down the situation. She smiles.

Caught red-handed.

'It's okay...I won't tell anybody,' she reaches for his hand and takes the conditioner bottle. 'that you use a mango-flavoured conditioner on your hair,' she bursts out laughing.

Mehreen returns and after a quick review of the situation begins laughing too.

'You're dating a gay,' she says to Arnika and there's more laughter.

'Okay stop,' he says grumpily. RED is the only colour visible on his face. He looks sheepishly at Arnika and she pulls his cheek.

'I know he's not gay,' she says looking directly in his eyes. That he isn't. Both the girls are sure of. His sister has seen the internet history on his laptop and his girlfriend has seen...well.

'You'd know better Arnika,' Mehreen comments merrily and all three of them continue laughing.

'Am I hallucinating or you both are actually laughing together?' his mother's voice echoes from downstairs, controlling the laughter overflow.

'You aren't hallucinating Ma...we have company,' Mehreen speaks on their behalf as Shadab signals them to go downstairs.

'Oh...who's there?' Ma's voice echoes again in the huge house.

'Bhai's friend...I mean Bhai's girlfriend,' Mehreen shouts back and Shadab playfully slaps her from behind. Arnika is naturally embarrassed.

Their mother is standing at the base of the staircase with a huge bouquet of lilies and petunias which she has picked up from the table in the living room.

'Mom....this is Arnika.'

'Arnika...Mom.'

Arnika smiles confidently and wishes his mother. His mother smiles back approvingly. Instant connect.

Shadab congratulates himself silently. He knew his mother would like her.

Her no makeup, straight hair, shorts and T-shirt, sweet voice and charming persona is just an add on.

'Beautiful flowers beta... Did someone tell you I like petunias?' his mother says, looking at Shadab.

'Oh...you got those flowers?' Shadab asks Arnika, surprised.

'Yes,' she replies a little slowly. There's still an air of unfamiliarity and it's suffocating her. 'I'd remembered when we'd gone to the botanical garden last week for sociology class that you'd told me that aunty likes petunias,' she ends.

'Wow...you have a sharp memory too,' his mother exclaims, taking her hands in hers. 'And Shadab tells me you've topped in the Economics test today.'

'Mom,' he groans as Arnika throws him a sharp glance.

His mother giggles.

'Okay beta...I think he doesn't want me to stay here anymore... I've got the kitchen arranged...Bhittal is there to help you both. Have fun...and thank you for the flowers,' she says and walks away with her daughter to her bedroom.

'So, you ready for your cooking class?' Shadab asks, as they walk to the kitchen.

'I guess,' she smiles nervously. Cooking has always had sad connotations in her life.

They reach the kitchen. Modular. Spacious. Reflecting his father's flourishing business.

Bhittal bhaiya, the family help, who has been in this house for more than a decade, welcomes them.

'Arnika...that's Bhittal bhaiya,' Shadab begins with the introductions again.

'We've met already...bhaiya opened the door for me,' she smiles at him. Shadab is relieved to see Bhittal bhaiya smile back in consent.

Rhea hadn't even acknowledged Bhittal bhaiya when she'd come home for the first time.

'Okay...so bhaiya...aprons,' Shadab says, clapping his hands.

The aprons arrive in no time. He knots the apron after she wears it. 'Gucci...pink,' he inhales her fragrance and whispers.

'I'm impressed,' she whispers back. Bhaiya's busy getting all the ingredients together.

'So Arnika…this is what you need,' Shadab begins. 'Around half-cup cocoa. The same amount of flour.' He picks up some flour from the bowl and brushes it on her nose. The old servant coughs to remind them of his presence. 'Yes…four egg whites…two teaspoon of vanilla essence…some Canola oil…half tablespoon baking powder.'

Arnika listens like an obedient student. 'I think I need to write all this somewhere,' she comments.

'Don't worry…I'll give you the recipe later,' he says and walks over to the fridge. 'What would you have?'

'Water,' she replies, scanning the ingredients, now all arranged properly by Bhittal bhaiya.

He walks back with the water bottle and pours her a glass of water before keeping the bottle on the marble slab, near the oven.

'Right…now we need to coat the baking pan with cooking spray.' He asks Bhittal bhaiya to get the pan and converts his words into action.

'Bhaiya, set the oven,' he instructs next and as Bhittal bhaiya turns around, he quickly plants a peck on her cheek.

'Shadab,' she hisses and regains her composure in no time as Bhittal turns around again.

Shadab's mind-mills begin to work. Bhaiya has to go.

He pretends he is looking for something in his pockets. 'Oh… my mobile phone,' he exclaims! 'Bhittal bhaiya, I think I've left my mobile in one of my jeans…can you go to my room and get it please…,' Shadab says and the poor, innocent servant obeys him and goes.

Shadab walks up to the door of the kitchen and after seeing that the door to his mother's room is closed, removes the door stopper and closes the door of the kitchen.

Arnika's stomach performs Olympic-level somersaults as she sees the door closed. Shadab grins at her, as he walks back, waving his cell phone.

'Mean guy,' she accuses him. 'Poor bhaiya.'

'It'll put him to some work at least...for a considerable time,' his voice is different. Seductively different.

'Umm...brownies,' she says to get him back on track.

'Oh yes...brownies...so where were we?' he asks, coming close to her.

She moves a little apart and says, 'Not so close for sure.'

Silence.

He's silent.

She's silent.

Then there's laughter.

It all begins with a smile. Metamorphosis into a subtle grin before changing to heavy guffaws, only to pull the reverse gear once again and shape back into simple smiles.

Then their eyes meet. Breathing increases.

Heads inch forward.

Their first kiss.

He tries not to be assertive. His lips gently brush hers.

She keeps her hand on the marble slab for support.

The next turns more passionate. It's a long kiss.

His hands trace her back.

She steadies herself and in the process, the water bottle falls.

They both break apart for a temporary moment. 'Leave that,' he whispers as their lips meet again. The water trickles down to the oven and the next second...BLAST!!!

Science calls it a short circuit. Sparks fly. Blue splinters. Yellow flames.

'FUCK! FUCK! FUCK! FUCK!' He says continuously as the

crackers continue to burst. Arnika begins to cough as the smoke engulfs them.

'What's happened?' His mother comes running into the kitchen and screams, followed by the servants.

One of the servants switches off the oven and finally, after some sincere efforts, the Diwali ends.

Their first kiss. Smoking hot. Electric, well literally!

seven

And the first time he meets her mother...he stammers, goes all red, hyperventilates and almost faints... So much for the practice.

9 August 2009

6 p.m.
'Mom, this is Shadab!'

'Shadab...Mom!'

'And then you give her the bouquet...remember she loves white roses...and then you wish her...flashing a very subtle smile... look at me,' she slaps Shadab lightly and continues, 'just the centre pair of teeth should be visible.'

'And how many times can I blink my eyes, Arni?' he mocks.

They both, after returning from the supermarket with all the necessities for the surprise dinner party for her mother, are seated in his car, parked in her driveway. Arnika's booked her mother for a spa. She wants her to be in her best mood when she meets Shadab for the first time that day.

'Shadab...get serious...I want Mom to get a good impression about you.'

'That...shouldn't be a cause for worry then, I'm a born charmer.'

'You're so humble,' she comments sarcastically and they both laugh.

'Fuck, I better get going,' she shrieks after looking at the little digital clock in his car and opens the door the next instant to get down. 'Don't forget to shave,' she shouts back as she starts to walk to the main door of her house.

'What all parts?' he questions from behind and smiles.

'Sick,' she shouts and closes the door. He reverses the car and whistling excitedly, thinks he's more than prepared for meeting her mother. Only if that was the case.

That night...

Be there at two... stay near the door.

Shadab messages Arnika at 9.15 p.m. She's pissed. He's late. Ritesh, Alisha, Bani, Vasu, Radhika and Stuti. Everybody's there except him.

Exactly two minutes later the doorbell rings.

'I'll get it,' Arnika shouts rather unnaturally and dashes to the door. Everybody in the living room, including her mother, is surprised at the sudden outburst.

Arnika opens the door only to find a huge bouquet of white roses uplifted in mid-air. Hundred and one, to be precise.

'Hi... Arni!' a familiar muffled voice from behind the bouquet is heard.

'Shadab,' she hisses and smiles at the same time. 'Idiot... let me help you,' she supports one end of the bouquet and they both juggle their way into the living room.

Ritesh is sharing a joke with everyone when Arnika and Shadab enter with the huge bouquet covering their faces. That awkward moment of silence begins. Spotlight is on them.

Naturally her mother is inquisitive about the guy who is literally hiding his face behind a wall of flowers with her daughter for company. She walks over to them as they keep the bouquet on the nearest table.

He's arranging a popped out rose back into the bouquet when her mother begins, 'And this must be…'

He turns around. As per the plan.

'Shadab…meet Mom,' Arnika says. As per the plan.

'Hello aun…OH MY GOD!' Shadab screams. Definitely NOT as per the plan. 'Ma'am…I…I'm a huge frigging fan of yours,' he feels sweat on his forehead and a little shiver run through his body. 'Arnika…Nishi Sinha is your mother…the Nishi Sinha… like wow…fuck, wow!'

Oops!

Profanity. Insanity. Her mother gets to hear and see it all. Arnika, redder than the tomato soup being cooked in the kitchen, looks down at her feet, not knowing what to say.

'Hi beta,' her mother finally says as Shadab tries hard to contract the still expanding grin on his face.

'GUYS,' he signals to everybody, who are as stunned as Arnika or her mother, to come near him. 'Since most of the people,' he clears his throat once everybody gets up and forms a little circle and continues, 'since most of the people in this room are ignorant souls, who have never given the beautiful world of theatre a chance, let me take this opportunity to introduce to you today one of the most gifted theatre artistes of this country.'

Arnika shoots a look in her mother's direction. She then realizes how silly it has been on her part to not tell Shadab who her mother is, especially before making them meet.

'She is not only a bestselling author, philanthropist, United

Nations worker and ma'am,' he bends down on his knees and asks for her visibly blushing mother's hand, 'a beautiful mother…happy birthday aunty.'

There's applause in the room. There are tears of happiness. In Arnika's eyes. A genuine smile on Nishi aunty's face. An excited gleam in Shadab's eyes.

Their first meeting. Well, not as planned. But, definitely better.

eight

And then they have their first fight…or do they?

2 September 2009

He calls her. Late night. She's busy on another call. Call waiting.

Reason enough to fight? Not really. There's ample scope for positive speculation. Could be a girlfriend. A cousin. Could be a guy, she's secretly dating…*naaa!* He disconnects the call.

Trust. It's like ice. Compact yet fickle enough to melt with a single crack. He trusts her.

That she doesn't answer his call that night and consequently doesn't sleep is a different story. Her cousin has had a break up. He's informed by her as soon as they meet the next morning.

Trust. Ice. Compact.

Fight avoided.

Virtue learned: Trust

23 September 2009

She's leaning against Ronil's desk. His arch rival. Engrossed. Laughing.

He walks into the class and calls for her. She responds in the negative. Continues laughing and talking.

Reason much to fight? Maybe...a little.

It's more of a gypsy version of a strong argument that happens that day during recess.

Virtue learned: A guy can't, repeat, can't stand his girl talk to someone he doesn't like. Space. It's more for the keyboard to have.

4 October 2009

She wants to spend some time alone. Doesn't feel like meeting him.

He wants just the opposite. Desperately.

She politely denies.

He enthusiastically persuades.

She loses her cool and screams at him.

He cuts the call.

Silence stabs.

She realizes her mistake after some time and calls to apologize.

Ego slaughter. Where's the fight then?

Virtue learned: Ego slaughter. Fight slaughter.

3 November 2009

Smoking. She thinks it's unhealthy.

He's addicted.

She hedges a kiss he's about to plant. Mouth fresheners are a limited solution.

He wants the kiss. Bad. It's that 'my way or the highway' moment for him.

She refuses point-blank.

Silence. Awkward silence.

The car is accelerated. The silence continues till he drops her back. The car screeches to a rude halt.

She gets down quickly and slams the door. Even ruder.

No goodbyes are exchanged. He drives off. In anger.

She walks away. In pain.

Do we see a proper fight here? If wishes were beggars, horses would ride. Love is a bitch. A stuck-up one at that. He drives back to her place after an enlightened stroke finds birth in his heart.

Repeated calls. Honks. Even the doorbell.

She finally comes out and sits in the car.

He drives to and parks his car in the secluded parking area of the sector's community centre.

Her eyes are red. The kohl is smeared. Faint brushes of liquid.

He takes out the pack of cigarettes.

Crushes it. Crumbles it. Opens the window. Throws it. Swears by her head. He'll try to quit.

He's rewarded. :-*

Virtue learned: It's okay to say sorry;
rewards follow generally.

nine

And that's how you know the relationship is going strong…

October 2009—May 2010

- When they both change their cellular talk plans, buy hands free to relax their heated ears from all the marathon conversations and Skype when it's getting too expensive.

- When their Facebook profiles say, *'In a relationship with…'* and every picture of them when uploaded gets the *'Awwws'*, *'so cute'* and *'touchwood'* comments and random likes.

- When she accompanies him for his haircut. And worse, he has to accompany her for her shopping trips.

- When he texts her without reason and calls her at 4 a.m. just to hear her voice.

- When every time the weather turns romantic or a romantic song plays anywhere around, they end up calling each other.

- When the guard, gardener, servant, cook in his house begin to recognize her.

- When they reach class late and his shirt is askew and her hair unsettled.

- When they both coincidentally get absent from the school on the same day.

- When he takes her mother for grocery shopping when her driver's not around.

- When her neighbours can recognize his car in her driveway.

- When COD (Call of Duty) is ignored for Twilight and 'I love you' is replaced by 'make me a sandwich'.

- When she's ready to kiss him even if he has had beer and he's content arguing with her on how she hasn't gained any microgram of weight, contrary to what she repeats every time he orders a chocolate cake.

- When he knows what brand of sanitary napkins she uses and she complains of how his cell phone and laptop are always full of porn.

- When she happily pays for them sometimes and he lets her drive his car. Risky. Still.

- When they fight over trivial issues, shout and abuse each other and yet at the end of the day, call and makeup. Communication. That's what keeps them going when they want it to work so badly.

- When his mother is happy for her son being taught Economics at the dining table.

- When her mother is glad that her daughter's softer side is sprouting. Moreover she's struck the balance between education and the 'non-academic' endeavours well. Rare. But has happened!

- When she goes to watch his plays along with her mother and repeatedly seeks her approval on his performance.

- When, at the ticket counter for a movie, he always asks for the centre corner seats and always sits on the right side to make sure her arm only brushes against his and no other guy's.

- When he waits outside the changing room, holding her bag as she tries a dozen dresses.

- When they both know all the passwords to each other's e-mail ids and social networking accounts.

- When she crumples every cigarette she finds in his car, in his room or in his pocket.

- When he disconnects her call for he can't pause his PlayStation and she pretends to be not hurt and realizes that he's a guy.

- When she remembers all the important anniversaries and he typically forgets them all and they fight. Flowers and chocolates don't help.

- When he buys her a Dairy Milk, not for her happiness but for the thrill he'd get when they both start biting the chocolate from the either ends.

- When she tells him to buy boxers because the briefs make him touch his crotch too often.

- When she learns to bake a cake for him on his birthday but fails miserably. Still, he sportingly takes a bite. Stomach suffers, but love thrives.

- When a look is enough for him to realize she's not okay even if she says otherwise.

- When she gets lectured by her mother over dinner on how it is important for her to know the boundaries and how it's the girl who always suffers later in life due to those 'weak' moments.

- When his father asks him over beer about how serious he is about her.

- When she forces him to spend time with his mother and talk to his Dad over the phone.

- When he wears the same shorts to their dates repeatedly. With the same set of boxers. Eeks.

- When she meets him on a bad 'hair' day. Proudly.

- When he checks out other girls in her presence and she selects the best of the lot for him.

- When she gets sloshed at a friend's party and he remains sober to handle her.

- When their phones have the same display picture. Of them.

- When the entire school knows they are going steady and strong.

- When the teachers bitch about them over tea and *samosas* in the staff room.

- When her call every morning serves as his alarm clock.

- When he starts getting possessive about her and asks her not to wear shorts to the gym and she snarls at him, reminding him of her space and they fight only to resolve it with the intervention of a common friend. She still wears the shorts and he the sulky expression.

- When they always get to sit on the back seats on a drive with friends.

- When they decide to limit their telephonic conversation as the pre-Boards approach.

- When she sets academic targets with ample rewards for him and he successfully completes them. Pleasure with business works.

- When they go to the extent of not talking beyond a fixed period during the Boards.

- When he helps her finish her college applications to the USA. A little scared, yet supportive.

- When she forces herself and comes out alive after seeing him kiss another girl for a play. It's just acting.

- When they start talking about their future. Devise plans. Think of ways to continue their relationship.

- When they both are ready to take the plunge for the phenomenon called LOVE.

ten

And those final moments together...even if it means he will accompany her on her shopping trips, make lists and prefer interaction over action and give up Lan gaming sessions with his friends for a chick flick...Yes, he has no other choice.

23 June 2010

What do you do when your girlfriend calls you to let you know she's coming over with a chick flick? Boring enough to make you appreciate trigonometry, especially just after you've had a word with your buddies and fixed a marathon Counter-Strike Lan gaming session for the same day.

You either impulsively decide to buckle that belt and refuse your girlfriend or simply tolerate the jeers from your buddies for your girlfriend's sake.

However, if you're in the likes of Shadab Parvez, you simply weigh the pros and cons of the situation with a cool mind.

The Home Theatre and DVD player is in your room. Your personal room.

With just one bed and perfect surround sound.

Moreover, chick flick equates to a sob-senti story.

Sob-senti story equates to her head on your shoulders every five minutes.

Her head on your shoulders every five minutes equates to you getting to stroke her hair carefully when carelessly your hand begins to stroke other entities, while you're busy watching the movie.

Or,

Lan gaming with friends equates to lots of beer and long hours of virtual action.

Dry, very dry.

Since reality supersedes virtual dilemmas ever more, you simply call up your buddies and tell them you've got to drive your mother to the doctor. It's an emergency. Slam the phone. Problem solved.

Ding dong!

Shadab is in the kitchen when the bell rings. No, he's not surprising her by fixing her a sandwich or baking her a cake. Even if she's flying to the US to join college in a few days, he's simply there to check if there are any breezers in the fridge, which can be smuggled to his room or he'll have to again steal his father's Vodka bottle from the bar.

It helps to have a father who's travelling most of the week for business and a mother, who rarely keeps a tab on mere bottles of alcohol in the fridge.

Shadab quickly fills the base of the bag with the breezer bottles.

He can hear Arnika and his mother laugh in the living room, as he continues to fill the bag with junk food packets and tinned snacks for their movie date.

A definite joke has been cracked at his expense and he realizes it only when the laughter continues to be heard.

He smiles momentarily before proceeding to the living room. It's always heart-warming for a guy to learn that his mother and his girlfriend get together even if it's at the guy's expense.

He walks up to the living room after sending the bag with the servant to his room, only to find his mother and her seated, pouring over a childhood album.

P.S.—His EMBARASSING childhood album.

More laughter continues.

'Mom,' he groans, 'this isn't fair... we had a deal that you won't show this album to anybody.'

'Hey... Shadab... I never knew you loved wearing polka-dotted underwear,' Arnika exclaims between the giggles.

'Mom!' Shadab screams and his mother closes the album the next instant.

Sorry beta... but look at you... you look so adorable. These pictures will be the only memories I have once you leave for college soon.'

Mothers and melodrama!

'Mom's been saying the same thing... all this while,' Arnika begins. 'I'm cooking for her tonight. She's so excited.'

'Beta... whenever you say things like these... I simply end up wondering what exactly did you see in my son?' his mother says dramatically, holding her hand.

Arnika winks at him as he continues to protest against the sudden rise of girl power.

'Right Mom... I'll cook for you tonight... and then take you to the doctor for food poisoning too,' he says in his defense.

More laughter and conversation continue for the next fifteen minutes. They threaten to extend further as his mother continues to hold her hand and discuss her preparations for college.

It takes Shadab some considerable effort in sign language and eye talk to make Arnika understand that the DVD player, the bed and the booze are waiting upstairs in his room.

His mother catches one such instance of eye talk. 'I think, I'm keeping you from some pre-planned activity.'

'Nno...not really...we were just planning to watch a movie,' Shadab tries hard to kill the excitement and sound casual.

'Oh...what genre?' his mother asks next.

'Action.' 'Romance.' They both say in the next second instantly and look at each other and smile nervously.

'An action-romance,' his mother rephrases the answer for them and smiles. Realizing she's certainly not invited, she gets up and calls for the servants.

'Nitu aunty...why don't you also watch the movie with us?' Arnika says with such earnestness that Shadab literally curses her at the speed of a million curses a second.

'Me?' she looks at Shadab, who switches to his all-smile mode. 'No...I need to meet my friends for lunch and then get the grocery...you people carry on.'

'Perfect,' he whispers. 'We'll order food from Dominos,' he adds in the next instant, already knowing what his mother would ask next.

'Right then...enjoy kids,' she says and leaves for her room.

'Enjoy,' is what Shadab repeats as he flashes Arnika a seductive smile.

Inside the room.

'DO. NOT. EVEN. THINK. ABOUT. IT,' Arnika says each word with clarity and force as she catches him stealthily turn the key in the lock, after she's entered his room.

'What?' his arms rise in protest.

'A few fucking days, Shadab...that's all we've got together...and all you can think about is…' There is a certain tinge of irritation in her voice.

'I was just checking if the key turns into the lock in this direction or not,' he protests.

'You weren't…you hormonal pig,' she accuses him.

'Fine…now you want to fight,' he says and jumps on to his bed.

'SICK,' she snarls at him.

'What…I can't even jump on to my own bed now?' The twinkle in his eye says the rest.

'I can't believe I'm with you,' she says, walking up to the TV cabinet and bending over to insert the DVD she's carrying with her in the DVD player.

'Me too,' he whispers, checking out her arse in her shorts.

'What did you say?' She instantly gets up and turns around.

'Me…I said…I just lust…I mean…just love you baby,' he winks at her.

'Shadab…please…there are things we need to talk about… issues which need to be discussed beforehand…I don't want this to end.' There is a sense of conviction in her voice, liquid in her eyes.

He gets up from the bed in a reflex action and takes the few steps that separate them and hugs her.

'I love you,' he combs her hair with his fingers and takes them behind her ears as she snuggles her face into his shirt. 'I can't think of losing you…ever.'

'You…have…not…even…taken…a bath,' she whispers between sobs and bursts out laughing.

'Bitch…you killed the moment again,' he says, still hugging her.

'You deserved this one,' she replies, breaking free from the embrace, 'Cologne and the deo…Mr Parvez…simply implies you haven't been in the shower since yesterday.'

'Well…you know me pretty well,' he replies and smiles.

'So, which movie do we get to see today?' he asks, walking back to the bed.

'*A Walk to Remember*,' she replies.

'Perfect. Full on sob story,' he thinks as he sets the pillows.

The odd ten-twelve times they've seen it together, it's inevitably ended in some action.

'What's there to eat?' she asks, walking back to the bed with the remote in hand.

'Me...and if you're vegetarian...there's some stuff in that bag on the study table,' he says, relaxing on the bed. 'What?' he questions after she shoots him a look.

'Be a man for once,' she murmurs within her teeth, as she walks to the table, gets the bag and walks back to the bed.

He's pulled the covers on to himself in a few seconds. Opportunist. That he is.

'It's not even cold...we don't need the blanket,' she says, unzipping the bag and taking out a chips packet.

'There's some booze too...in the bottom...if you want it... that is,' he says, avoiding the question.

'No...not right now.'

She claps loudly and the lights turn off. Sensor lighting. Saves the effort.

She snuggles on to him and switches the movie on.

Some twenty minutes later.

'What's the time difference between New York and New Delhi?' she asks, resting her head on his chest.

No reply.

'You slept again!' she elbows him after she gets up and finds him sleeping.

'Hey!!' he gets up with a start. 'Wow! That's a nice scene,' he tries hard to cover up.

'FUCK YOU!' there's anger in her voice.

'Oh come on Arnika...we've seen this movie twelve times.'

'Eleven,' she corrects him.

'Yes...eleven...I'm bound to get sleepy,' he rubs his eyes.

'Even when I'm in such close proximity?' the way she says it, believe you me, it can give a dead old man the meanest hard on ever.

'Well,' he looks at her top.

Direct gaze.

Unabashed.

'What are you looking at?' she asks, getting up.

'Your heart,' he replies back.

Smooth bitch, he is.

She hugs him the next second.

'By the way...there's a difference of eight and a half hours between Delhi and New York,' he says softly.

'You weren't sleeping?' she asks, amazed.

'I was just soaking in your presence...won't get this Gucci perfume's fragrance on my shirt so often now.'

There's a sudden silence.

'Promise me, you'll never leave me,' Mandy Moore says in the background.

'I promise you,' the guy in the movie replies.

They both kiss.

In the movie.

In the room.

24 June 2010

Shopping.

Guys find the very word and the whole idea as sick and useless as the code of honour, PlayStation, football and bear hugs, butt slaps, complicated Hi5s are for girls. Guys are best at simple impulsive buying, like throwing all flavours of Orbit chewing gum in the shopping cart and not fussing over the best because it's just chewing gum after all! Like buying a T-shirt without trying it, just because they believe it'll fit them even as they see it hanging from a distance. While girls love to surf, scrutinize, put the salesgirl to tedious work, cluster around a hundred T-shirts, spend light years in the trial room and then finally reject the chosen apparel because it's apparently highly priced or it doesn't conceal a faint brush of fat at the right place.

It's more like the 'hunter-gatherer' syndrome. Girls tend to gather by meticulously looking all over and planning for later harvest, etc. while guys hunt down one deal, run it down and go home to play with it (like it's a bison for dinner, baby).

Guys are result oriented, so is Shadab.

Girls are process oriented, so is Arnika.

Evidently, she's carrying two shopping lists, one for herself and the other for the guy who has been pestering her to stop at every coffee or electronics shop as they set out on a crusade in Sector 17—a shopping hub in Chandigarh—to buy off stuff she would need in college.

Shadab's carrying a handful of handbags!

They've ticked almost everything that is on her precise yet diverse list.

Arnika's shopping list:

- ♥ A pairs of jeans
- ♥ A nice pair of stilettos
- ♥ A formal skirt
- ♥ A dress—a very short dress (yes, she's written that along)
- ♥ Some sexy lingerie

It's been a pain mostly, the only good part being he getting to select her lingerie, even if he really won't get to see her in it most part of the year.

'Wow...this is tiring,' Arnika exclaims after she completes her stroll in the new Esprit store, without a cause.

'Tell me about it,' Shadab spits slight venom as his stomach grumbles and he struggles with the handbags.

He's not the guy who would open doors and pull out chairs or carry a handkerchief, yet he's doing it for her.

It's special this time.

Her flight is in ten days.

'Awwww...not my fault...somebody wants to act all macho suddenly and carry the bags even when the girl has asked him twice to hand some over,' she pulls his cheek softly.

'I want you to remember this day...until we get to shop like this again,' his voice is too emotional, too alien for the light moment.

She's quiet.

He's quiet.

A slight blink of liquid. She won't let it pour further. They knew this would happen one day.

'Let's get you some nourishment Princess Shadab and then we can start with your list.' Her arm encircles his arm and he looks at her and fights the intense urge to kiss her in the market.

'Yes...Ms Kill-the-moment-with-your-sad-humour,' he replies and they both start walking towards the nearest restaurant.

At the restaurant.

He opens the door. A few minutes later, he pulls up a chair too for her.

'Am I in Narnia…or has your body been inhabited by a chivalrous alien?' she jokes as he sits down, not opposite but next to her.

He wants to be close to her, reduce the distance for the one last time.

They look into each other's eyes, hoping the moment would stay. Permanently.

Trying to find their reflection in each other's eyeballs, a small yet confident picture of them.

'Good afternoon sir and madam…water…bottled or regular?' The waiter breaks the moment.

'Anything that'll be sufficient to drown you,' he murmurs and she laughs, while signalling to the amused waiter to get water.

Lunch is ordered next. Chinese. Now his favourite too.

She cools the soup for him. It might be their last together until they meet in December. Her lips touch the spoon softly as she blows bouts of cold air on it. He drinks it from the very same spot that has her lips' imprint.

The dish bowls are polished in no time. They've crossed the stage of having careful bites at a date so that they don't appear to be hungry devils to each other, a long time back.

'Dessert?' he asks her as the waiter clears the table.

'Only if you were on the menu,' she winks at him.

The waiter blushes.

'Could that arrangement be made?' he asks the already embarrassed waiter.

'Shadab!!' she hits his arm playfully. 'Cheque,' she says. The waiter quickly walks away and brings the bill at the same speed. He's probably scared of their intentions.

'Sir,' he holds it out for Shadab. He's just about to take it when Arnika steals it from his hand.

'And this is?' Shadab demands.

'My treat,' she simply says, sending her mother's credit card for another swipe journey.

'And the occasion?' he asks, taking out her credit card from the cheque copy and keeping his inside.

'I think I've realized today that you're the best thing that has happened to me in my life and I need to celebrate this feeling.'

The waiter grunts softly to let them know he's still there.

She slides her card back in, takes out his and hands it over to him. The waiter leaves.

'Back to your shopping list,' she says with a sigh.

'Don't go na,' he says suddenly.

Hollow words. She prefers to stay silent.

'Let's go,' she says, once the waiter is back. She won't look into his eyes now. They make her self-control go weak.

'Let's go,' he repeats what she's said.

This won't hurt much...they'd get used to the idea of being away...
yes...perhaps...maybe...will they?

25 June 2010

Lists.

Why do girls love to make 'do and do not' lists for their guys? Why do they even pretend to take their boyfriend's suggestion when in the end they won't budge an inch from what they've decided?

Why do guys let all of this happen? Perhaps it's because deep down, Pacific deep down, they know girls are more rational, emotionally stable and definitely better decision makers. That they never accept or portray the facts is a different story altogether.

'Shadab…can you stop texting and listen to me?' Arnika says angrily. They are in a CCD (Café Coffee Day), located at a stone throw away from her house.

She's got her laptop along. Yes, for typing out the do's and don'ts for him, once she leaves for the US.

'Yes…say,' he continues to tap the keypad of his Blackberry Bold without looking up. Cricket is more important than conversations; when will girls understand?

'Listen, I need to be back in another thirty minutes…Mom's been complaining on how you've become more important to me than her…I need to spend time with her too…so if you could stop checking the score every two seconds and…' she's interrupted by the waiter as he brings in their order.

A single slice of chocolate fantasy cake. Two cappuccinos. The brew on her's bearing a chocolate heart.

He's asked the waiter to get one made at the time of ordering. Like always.

Arnika looks at the waiter briefly. Regular college student. Cute enough to raise Shadab's head and kill his romance with the mobile.

'Hey…I haven't seen you around…just joined in?' Arnika

questions the waiter in her most friendly tone.

Shadab's fingers cease, head rises. The mobile goes in the pocket. Immediately.

'Yes ma'am,' the waiter, surprised at the sudden warmth by the hot chick sitting next to, probably, her boyfriend, replies softly.

She takes a sip from her coffee. Shadab's curious.

'Oh...Dinesh,' she reads his name plate and smiles, 'could you get some more sugar?' she rolls her eyes briefly. The waiter is all smiles. He goes back to the counter.

Shadab picks up her coffee and takes a sip.

'The sugar's fine,' he says candidly.

'Oh is it?' she fakes the damsel look so well. 'I must have not noticed,' she winks at him.

Jealousy works. Big time. Always.

'Okay fine...'

This time he's cut by the waiter.

'Ma'am,' he offers her the sugar pouches.

'I'll take that,' Shadab almost snatches the pouches from the waiter's hand while Arnika flashes him an apologetic smile. He walks back to the counter, confused.

'Fine...now that you've almost burned me to bits...tell me.'

'Ouch. Jealousy,' she giggles yet again and opens her laptop screen, presses a few keys and opens the Microsoft Word.

She gives the page a heading and shows him.

Do's & don't's to be followed by Shadab Parvez & Arnika Sinha.

'You have to be kidding me,' he raises his hand to protest.

'I'm serious about this...about us...if you're not,' she pretends to close her laptop screen.

'No...stop it Arni...you know I don't need this,' he says, holding her hand and stopping her from shutting the screen.

'We do Shadab...let's be practical about this, okay? We are eighteen...Goddamn eighteen...I mean...we don't even know what we want in our lives at the end.'

'Talk about yourself.'

He's hurt. He knows what he wants. Her.

She ruffles his hair playfully. 'I know baba...it's just that...we need to decide on a few things beforehand.'

'Like?' he scoops a bite from the slice of cake.

'Okay,' her fingers are on the laptop keyboard. She gives a subheading to the page and numbers the next word she types.

The subheading.

We always need to (do's):

1. Trust each other
'Right...that means if I upload a picture on Facebook of me and a hot, sexy girl falling all over me at an in-house party or something... you would understand that she's just a friend,' he says after reading the first clause.

'Yes...just like if you call me at one in the night and some American guy answers your call...you won't throw a fit...he's just a friend,' she replies.

Tit for tat. Edges meet, not collide. 1-1 to each of them.

2. Communicate
She types in next.

'That will not be an issue,' he says confidently. 'We will post on each other's Facebook walls regularly...Skype every day plus there is the Blackberry messenger... I love technology,' he concludes.

'Yes... and I've strategized it all for us... my college would finish at two in the afternoon and I'll be back in the hostel at say, maximum by 3 p.m.... so,' her eyes shrink into slits as she calculates the time difference.

He smiles at this. Love.

'NY is eight and a half hours behind Delhi, so you can give me a call at midnight or something,' she adds.

'Okay and you need to tell me everything about your life... no scope for speculation and we will video chat the way I want... sometimes,' he grins.

'Sick,' she mutters.

'Come on, I'm a normal guy... I have needs,' he takes another bite of the chocolate cake and licks the chocolate around his lips with his tongue.

'You really didn't need to be all that suggestive,' she says, adding, 'getting back to the list...'

He cuts in.

'Wait... can we order something else too... I'm hungry.'

'God,' she says exasperatedly, 'you're such a guy... all you need is food, sex and sleep.'

'Err... you forgot cricket and PlayStation,' he replies meekly and quickly turns his head to call the waiter.

The same waiter comes. This time he's looking down.

He orders.

'Two choco lattes, a chicken sandwich and a chocolate brownie and umm... should be all.'

'Make that one choco latte... I'm leaving,' her voice is cold.

'No wait,' he holds her arm and turns his head to the waiter and signals, 'two'.

The waiter grumbles and goes back.

'Oh...where's the laptop?' he asks earnestly.

'In my bag,' she replies sourly.

'Take it out. We need to complete the list. You're not even concerned about us anymore. Seriously Arnika,' he imitates her tone.

'I can't believe I'm with you,' she mutters under her breath as she takes out the laptop again and opens it.

'Me too,' he says very softly.

'I heard that,' she says sarcastically.

'Yes...Arni...I obviously did not deserve somebody like you...I mean, look at you...perfection personified...look at me.'

She interjects.

'Pain in the arse personified.'

The smiles are back.

It always works. Making your girl believe she's the better person of the two. Using heavy adjectives and oh yes, that little liquid in the eye. Perfect.

The waiter returns with the order.

Shadab begins to open the ketchup pouch with his teeth.

'Such a guy...give it to me,' she snatches the pouch from his hand and uses her delicate fingers with acute precision. The result. Fingers work better than the teeth.

'Yes...so...the list,' he says, taking a big bite from the chicken sandwich.

'Right,' she takes a quick sip off the latte and begins to type again.

3. Give space

He begins to say something but she stops him and starts, 'All I mean by giving space to each other is that...the last one year we've been together for almost ten hours a day...things would change now… everyday calling does not mean you call me after every fifteen minutes and start crying and howling… oh baby, I miss you… please come back…,' she dramatizes the dialogue in the end.

'Okay,' he says simply. Chicken sandwich is obviously more important than a list which he knows they won't really follow.

'Perfect,' she smiles. This is going easier than she'd thought.

4. Try to be supportive of each other
'But we are pretty supportive,' he concludes, licking his fingers.

'A. Stop that.'

'B. Remember the time when I said I want to learn Salsa in school and the teacher paired me with Anmol, who threw a tantrum despite being repeatedly asked to join me in the first place. But, no, somebody won't give up football for that! Also hang on, remember the time when I wanted to get my hair coloured… who was the one to throw a fit… and the parking-lot fight… the poor guy had accidentally hit me.'

'But Anmol's a pervert, the hair colour would have sucked and the driver needed to learn how to take care of machines.'

'I wouldn't have let him touch me beyond necessity and the hair colour was to be my decision…,' she takes a deep breath before continuing, 'listen… all of this worked because I did not want to hurt you or anger you but now… once I'm away… I hope you understand.'

She looks into his eyes. Deep.

'So it's okay if I shave off this stubble and get an eyebrow piercing?' he asks excitedly.

'No. That'll just make you look gay… actually in retrospect… do whatever you want… at least I won't be thinking of girls hitting on you then,' she laughs.

He pretends to be hurt.

'Okay...let's begin with the do not's,' she says.

'No wait...I want to add another point in the do's.'

'What?' she asks confused.

He turns the laptop towards him and types.

5. No remembering special dates. No fighting over what I wear. No lectures on studying. Lots of cyberse...

She steals the laptop from his hand, not letting him complete.

'Anything else?' she asks.

'Yes,' he says.

'What?' pin-sized irritation in her voice.

'I love you.'

He looks into her eyes.

She looks back.

It's their favourite game.

He always loses.

Her smile that follows is his actual win.

Her cell phone rings and she's the one who ends up losing today.

'Hello...Hi Mom! Yes...just leaving...I know, Mom.'

He continues looking at her, trying to capture every little inch of her. The hair, straight naturally. The kohled eyes, serene. The sharp nose, the deep neckline, the high cheekbones, the sleek lips. Everything.

She snaps her fingers in front of his eyes and he rises out of the trance.

'What?' she asks smiling.

'Nothing,' he looks down.

'Okay...I need to rush now...I think the do's are enough...the don'ts are just the opposite of it...I'll mail you a copy,' she keeps the laptop in her bag, takes a large slurp of the latte and signals the waiter for the cheque.

'Don't go,' he says suddenly.

'I have to...Raashi aunty is home...she's leaving for Singapore tomorrow...I need to meet her.'

The waiter arrives with the cheque.

'I got that,' she takes it from him. He's too pensive to argue or deny her today.

'Let's move,' she gets up, after paying the waiter.

'Don't go,' he repeats again.

'I told you...I have to...now move...quick,' she holds him by his shoulder. He gets up. They go to his car and he drives her to her house.

'Don't go,' is what he says even when she kisses him on his cheek as she gets out of the car.

'I have to...aunty.'

He cuts in.

'Just stay here...I love you.' His voice is calm. Too calm—this coming from him. It's got a deep meaning.

She closes her eyes for a brief second. Takes a deep breath. 'Bye,' she says and turns around, jogs to her gate and goes inside... without looking back at him.

eleven

And it's time for the final farewell and to take the relationship to the next level.

2 July 2010

Dim lights. Soft music. A rarely cleaned room, cleaned today and scented to perfection. Heart-shaped balloons on the walls. A large greeting card which says 'Miss You', placed right in the centre of the room. Rose petals on the floor in abundance. Unlit candles, for he's obviously not letting anyone enter his room beforehand. Arnika is fully aware of where all of this will end, as soon as she enters Shadab's room and sees all of this.

There's a faint brush of dying sunlight escaping from the spaces between the curtains. It's six in the evening. Their last day together, before she flies off to the US next morning, has been pretty eventful till now.

Breakfast with his parents.

They've gifted her a gold chain and a Mont Blanc pen, which she's profusely tried to refuse.

His parents love her a lot.

Shadab's been more focused, more determined, more serious about school, education, life, ever since she's entered the scene.

Moreover, they are simply elated that the children haven't been inspired from the Bollywood sagas, where teens, soaked in puppy love, decide to get married and forget normal basic procedures of life, like career and education.

The parents from both sides have tried to be friends, mentors, guides—flexible yet firm in their decisions and guidance. The mothers on both the sides did not go into a fit when they came to know about the children and their feelings. His father himself has slept every night with his girlfriend since the last twenty-two years. Shadab's eighteen. Also, if you haven't been able to figure it out yet, that girlfriend is his mom.

After breakfast, he drops her back to her house and picks up Ritesh, not before booking his mother for a movie show in the evening with her friends, ensuring she returns late and double checking with his father's secretary of a dinner meeting with a client. They both then come back to his place, en route a brief visit to the chemist to set up his room for the evening. It's supposed to be special; it's supposed to be their first time.

'You know how to use it, right? There's a whole procedure to be followed,' Ritesh asks him in earnest.

'Yes...I googled it up and then I've practised it too.'

They both Hi5 each other and get back to setting up the apparatus for the experiment to follow and after making sure the room looks just its part, they both quickly get ready to go for her farewell lunch.

After tearful goodbyes and sob tales, servings of laughter, slices of remembrances and memories, sprinkles of nostalgia and loads of tequila shots and rum balls, he drives her back to his house.

Bani, her closest friend has gifted her a Chanel perfume, a mug bearing their picture, a Swiss knife and pepper spray.

'You'll need this...today...if he gets too harsh,' she's whispered in her ear. The giggle that has followed did not go unnoticed by him. Arnika has obviously not brought that along to the room.

'I love you.'

His breath on her shoulder feels hot. Familiar yet unsettling.

She's ready for it. It's called taking the relationship to the next level. It's a symbol of being together for moments, to leave an imprint for a lifetime.

His hands encircle her waistline from behind, as her bare neck in the halter feels the touch of his lips.

She turns around and hugs him. Intense. Hungry.

'I love you.'

He says it again, this time caressing her hair. She's closed her eyes. He raises her chin. The lips meet. Soft. Lyrical. Almost like a feather brushes upon the surface of water.

The kiss is different today. More of emotion, less of hormone.

His hands reach for the hem of her skirt. A sudden shyness takes over. This isn't the first time they've felt each other, yet today seems to be different.

'Promise me you won't forget me… won't ever break my trust,' she says as their lips part momentarily.

'I won't,' he huffs. This time the kiss is more passionate. Almost hungry. Their tongues collide with a fiery streak. 'I can't… I love you.'

'Good… otherwise it'll be my Swiss knife and your…' she suddenly says.

They both burst out laughing.

'Arnika… what the… this was supposed to be intense,' he complains.

'Yeah?' she questions, unzipping her top for him. 'Like this?' she asks, the naughty smile intact.

'*Na*… like this,' he takes off his pants. SpongeBob boxers. Her favourite.

'I know you won't have it with anyone else,' she says with much conviction, as they sit on his bed. 'Not because I trust you or something, but because once any girl sees these boxers... she'll simply run away.' More laughter.

This isn't how it should be. They both should be nervous, scared to pee.

He decides it's time to give her the final surprise. He knows she'll get blown away by it. It's been painful, hard to get but in the end, it's all been in the name of love... his love for her.

He gets up from the bed and stands on it.

'What?' she demands. 'Let me make one thing very clear... I'm not trying any weird positions... let it be simple... just the way it should be,' she ends up seductively.

'There's a final surprise for you Arnika... to let you know that even if you're going to be a thousand miles away... you'll always be close to my heart.' He takes off his T-shirt in the next instant only to reveal her name tattooed permanently on his bare chest, just next to his heart.

Her voice chokes. This wasn't supposed to be so hard. She'd always made sure there is a line between them, yet he's gone the extra mile to erase it.

'I love you,' she pulls him back on to her. 'I fucking love you, Shadab Parvez.' And then they make love. It's not sex.

And that's a wet night... well, literally liquid!

'Don't go,' is the first thing that Shadab says as soon as she picks up his tenth call in the last two hours.

'Okay,' she whispers back hurriedly. Her mother's sleeping with her today. A sudden burst of motherly love has probably happened after she got her first period.

Walking again to the washroom is not a good option. She's been there six times, just to let him know how much she would miss him too.

'Please...can you sneak out for five minutes,' he literally pleads.

'Shadab,' she pulls the covers on her face, 'it's 3 a.m. in the night...my flight is in the next four hours...Mom's sleeping with me,' she feels her Mom stir.

'So?' he's ready to ignore all reason today.

'So...I cannot come out right now...you're already driving us to the airport tomorrow...what's the worry?' her voice is the lightest whisper. There's no response from his side.

The night is still.

A faint sound of music murders the silence.

His sentimental playlist again.

'I...love...you,' his voice is interjected by sobs. It's acceptable for boys to cry over the most loved toys.

'Are you crying? You'd promised me you won't.' The realization pierces the deepest core of her heart. Prickling pain. She feels her eyes turn moist.

'Nnoo...I'm not...crrr...yyinggggg.' The emotion dam's just burst. There's an overflow on both sides of the receiver. It takes some hour-like minutes to tap the water.

'It's just a matter of six months...and then you know, we both will Skype every day...and we also have our Blackberry messengers...it won't be all that difficult,' she tries to assure herself rather than him.

Technology today is like medicine to the wounded hearts. Cheap. Affordable. Easily available. Result oriented.

'Yes...listen, I think you should sleep now...it's a long flight... you need rest...I'll be there at 6 a.m....give me a call once you're up...I've to pick up Bani and Ritesh on the way too.' It takes him courage equivalent to the weight of a boulder to say all of it, yet he knows it's important. He needs rest himself. There's a lot to be done tomorrow once she's gone. His college also starts next week.

'Shadab…I love you baby,' she says with all the emotions she can muster, with her mother sleeping inches away.

He remains silent. Instead, she hears a song playing from his end—

Leavin on a jet plane. (John Denver, 1966)

> *All my bags are packed, I'm ready to go*
> *I'm standin' here outside your door*
> *I hate to wake you up to say goodbye*

A tear drops from her eye and ends its journey into her pillow, when she hears the last line and cuts the call.

This won't be easy for them.

Yet. They still want it.

Love can wait. Life has to happen.

twelve

For it's adieus...and never goodbye.

5 July 2010

The airport—Every love story has it. It's a strange place. A platform to opportunity; a pilgrimage of separation.

Luggage trolley—The guy always pulls it for the girl, even if the porter is just a hundred bucks and a call away.

Sunglasses—That's what the guy has to wear to not let the world know how red the eyes get from crying. There's obviously more room for the redness.

A bouquet of red roses—The girl holds them securely. Close to her heart. It's what she will keep with her in the flight, taking out one rose from the bunch and preserving it in a book for years.

A minute in the washroom—Is what the girlfriends need with each other. Last minute hugs, quick advices and a little makeup and touch-up.

Coffee—Is what the guy gets for the girl's mother as they all sit in the waiting lounge.

A little advice—Is what the girl's mother gives to the boy. These years are meant to shape one's future. Words like hard work, grit, determination and passion are thrown later.

A kiss on the forehead—Is again reserved for the girl's mother to the boy. It's her time to acknowledge his regard for her, his love for her daughter, his sadness for her happiness.

Excitement—Is just not what the girl feels despite this being the beginning of a dream much awaited.

Boarding call announcement—Is just what the guy never wants the speakers to blurt. Unavoidable.

Tears—Every farewell thrives on it. The guy, despite being one, is permitted to shed a few. The girl has full liberty to smudge the little kohl gracing her eyes.

Hugs—A symbol of warmth, of shared chemistry. The girl gets one from her best friend, one from her boyfriend.

Kiss on the cheek—The maximum you can do, if you're a girl and your Mom's standing right next to your boyfriend.

A moment together—Is what the mother luckily gives them, when she boards the flight early after saying, 'Come soon'.

Some tissues—Is what the guy uses to rub off the smudged kohl on the girl's fair face. It's the touch that matters. His fingers, her cheek.

Eye contact—The girl and the guy avoid it. It'll screw up the 'put-up brave' act.

A farewell hug—Is what the guy gives before the girl realizes. It's finally time to say goodbye.

A pat on the back—Is what the guy gets from his best friend as they see her walk through the door.

A solitary tear.
A heavy heart.

A song—That plays in the boy's car, on the way back.

So kiss me and smile for me.
Tell me that you'll wait for me.
Hold me like you'll never let me go.

thirteen

And love has a hangover…their first day apart.

9 July 2010 (IST)

Buzzzzzzzz.

He stirs a little.

Buzzzzzzzzzzzzzzzzzzzzzzz.

He tosses.

Buzzzzzzzzzzzzzzz buzzzzzzzzzzzz buzzzzzzz.

It takes him a quantum of effort to open his eyes and search for his phone in his bed. He finally finds it after two minutes as the buzz continues. Accustomed by habit, he begins.

'Yes I got up!! Arni—,' he stops. It's not the same any more. The voice on the other end is different. She's gone.

'Morning or should I say afternoon Shadab,' his mother says with mild humour and the mirage crumbles down to reality. With one hand on his throbbing head, he looks at the wall clock.

1.30 p.m.

'Yyes…Hi Mom!' he replies, after a long pause as he tries hard to remember when exactly had he fallen asleep.

Was it when he was being counselled and consoled by Ritesh

and Alisha on the phone?

Was it when he was waiting for her to call from Germany, her transit halt?

Was it when he was watching their pictures in his laptop. 1.4 GB worth of pictures?

Was it when he was downloading new sentimental songs?

'Shadab…Shadab…slept again?' his mother's voice pops his bubble of thoughts and brings him back to the present. Without Arnika.

'Yes…I mean…no…I…mean…how long have I been sleeping for?' he asks foolishly.

His mother smiles into the phone. It's a helpless smile. She's given birth to him. She knows every pulse, every beat of his heart.

'Why don't you get up and come down for lunch? We could talk,' she offers carefully.

His stomach grumbles at the very mention. 'Okay,' he says and hangs up to look at the display screen of his cell phone. Longingly. Their picture.

Seven missed calls. There's a notification at the rear end of the screen. He quickly opens the log, fearing the worst.

FUCK. MOUNTAINS. OCEANS. SEAS—of it.

Four missed calls belong to an international number with a code he doesn't recognize. He's not been to Germany either.

He tries calling back. Doesn't get through.

Dejected, he gets up and almost falls back on to the bed.

Wobbly knees.

Skipped dinner. Cried.

Slept through breakfast. Sulked.

And then they say love makes you go weak in the knees. Reason enough.

10 July (India), 9 July (Pacific Ocean) 2010.

She breathes an exasperated whiff of air on to the little glass window of the plane, as it smoothly crusades over the Pacific Ocean.

Her mother's asleep in the adjoining seat.

The mist appears momentarily as the air particles collide against the glass and her fingers quickly trace his name. It disappears even before she can smile.

Every breath she takes is taking her away from him, literally!

She sighs at seeing the name fade. Shadab did not answer her calls from the payphone at the Frankfurt Airport some hours back.

'He must be sleeping,' she had concluded with a little sorrow and gone back to her mother.

It's not like they haven't ever witnessed a day when they haven't heard from or about each other, but this time, it's different.

Deep down. Valley deep down, she knows this is just the beginning to what will be different. Difficult.

'Ma'am...can I get you something?' An airhostess, bound by duty to comfort the insomniac passengers, while the rest of the plane sleeps, walks up to her quietly and asks.

'No,' she smiles, 'I'm good.'

'You sure?' This time, her tone is more personal.

Arnika looks at her. Twenty something. Pretty. Well dressed. Like any other airhostess yet her smile is not plastic.

'I know I look like a terrorist here...lonely...withdrawn... awake...but I'm good.'

The airhostess shoots her a genuine smile and turns around

to go but is stopped by her voice.

'Actually...*could I get a chocolate brownie?*' she hears Shadab's voice bounce in her mind and her vocals echo it.

'Right,' she smiles and walks back.

Her mother stirs a little and she covers her shoulder with the blanket. After doing so, she retreats back to breathing again on the glass window.

Tracing his name again.//
Watching it disappear.//
Yet again.

fourteen

And their first video call...they talk...they discuss...they make good use of technology...very good use.

11 July 2010

11 p.m. Indian Standard Time. India.

    1.30 p.m. Eastern Standard Time. New York.

    Is when she comes online on Skype and video calls him.

    Their first conversation. Finally.

    He's been arranging his clothes in his new cupboard in Delhi, when the laptop's speakers come alive, signalling her call.

    Yes. He's shifted. Along with Ritesh to a plush apartment in Saket. His college starts in two days. Ritesh's already has.

    And to celebrate that quite aptly, he's gone to meet Alisha, who's also shifted to a PG accommodation in Kamla Nagar.

    'Hel...lo,' he pants after he dashes to his bed and answers the dying call. The inbuilt video cameras in both the laptops verse them with each other.

    'Hey!!!!' she shrieks in excitement as she sees him on her laptop screen.

    Live.

    'Hi baby! Hold on for a second,' he replies, wrestling with the wires of his headphones which have intertwined and formed a new Kamasutra position.

    'Oh my God! I've missed you...so FUCKING missed you...

how have you been? Have you shifted? I tried calling you from Germany and you were probably sleeping or something…how's Delhi? How's aunty? Did she cry at the time of your leaving? Have you begun college? What's with your Facebook status? You look tired…have you been smoking? God!! There is so much to talk about…and what's with your hairstyle?'

'Arnika. Breathe,' he plugs the headphones into the laptop, embraces them around his ears and continues, 'you look pretty and I…I love you,' he ends very softly.

'I love you too,' she whispers back.

An unnatural silence clouds over the situation.

'Arnika I…,' Shadab begins, but is cut midway.

'Where's Ritesh?'

'Thank you for not letting me complete and killing the emo-moment yet again…Ritesh is probably screwing his girlfriend who lives in the same city and doesn't kill the emo-moments every time,' he says sarcastically.

'No problem…we could find you one too.' That's one comeback.

'Where's aunty?' he doesn't want to start an argument.

She always wins.

'She's gone with Ritu aunty to buy me a local SIM card, we could BBM then.'

'Ritu aunty?'

'Yea…Mom's friend. She's staying with her. It's better than the parent dorm here.'

'Oh okay…So, how's the college…How's the crowd?'

'Amazinggggg.'

'Does amazinggggg include boys?'

'HOTT boys…there's variety.'

'Yeah?'

'Yes…one of them asked me out for coffee too, yesterday.'

'Oh, okay.'

There's a faint prick in his heart. Very faint. Like a mild, soundless fart. But. Fuck, it pains!

'Wow... Mr Parvez, it's not even been a week and you're already jealous.'

'You think so?' the emotions inside betray his put up tone. Being an actor helps. But. Not when you're in love.

'I know so!'

'Right.'

He changes his position and lies down on the bed, the webcam now giving her a full view of his boxer-clad hairy legs and loose T-shirt.

'So Arnika Sinha... won't you show me your room?'

'Shadab Parvez, realizing the connotations attached with what you've just said and your convenient repositioning... I'd rather not,' she says with a straight face.

'But why?... It's not like I'm taking off my T-shirt or something... especially like this,' he takes off his T-shirt the next instant.

ARNIKA

The name's etched on his chest. Permanently.

It lights up her eyes.

'You like what you see... don't you Arni?' he says, tracing his fingers along her name on his bare chest.

'Yyou know thiss... this isn't fair,' she says half-heartedly. It's afternoon and getting virtually compatible isn't really a healthy option, yet the battle's almost lost for her.

She knows. He knows.

He inches forward and focusses the webcam on his boxers.

'Shadabb,' she groans. 'Please... can we just talk today?'

'But we are,' he says, not budging his webcam view, even by an inch.

'Yes...talk while seeing each other's FACES.'

'Okay. Whatever you say,' he inches forward again and brings the webcam focus back to his face.

'So...you really want to see my room?' she questions.

'Sure.'

She gets up from her bed, the laptop in her hand and moves around the limited four by four in-campus hostel room.

'That is the cupboard...that's the view from my room's window...that's the door to the washroom...that's my bed, that's my...'

'Stop,' he cuts her.

'What happened?' she asks, surprised.

'Turn the webcam back to the bed,' he says with intent.

'Umm...okay,' she does as instructed.

'Now...shift towards the left, a little...yes a little more,' he says and she complies. 'A little...yeah PERFECT,' he whispers and smiles.

'Huh...oh okay,' she too smiles as they both end up looking at the photo frame bearing their picture on her bedside table. 'This way the first thing I'd see every morning would be us,' she ends.

'I love you.' Three words. A thousand emotions.

'I love you too.'

She says as she continues the visual encounter, showing him her washroom, the inside of her cupboard and the books she'll have to slog through.

Free campus Wi-Fi is definitely an added advantage to her mobile love story. Pun intended.

'Okay...now it's your turn to show me your apartment,' she says, sitting on her bed, once she's finished.

'Erm...Arni...we haven't really unpacked.'

It's a lie. His first, unassumingly though. He doesn't have her picture anywhere in the whole apartment. The fact that Angelina Jolie and a few others of her rank and stature have already adorned the walls of his washroom, which he would have to include in his tour, definitely doesn't help.

Moreover, his apartment, though bigger, is by all means shittier and more untidy than hers. Cardboard boxes on the floor. Unmatched curtains and cushions. Yesterday night's pizza leftovers on the kitchen slab, Ritesh's underwear spread on the chair in the dining area.

Shadab's promised her on trying to make a sincere effort to get more sophisticated than a pig and he doesn't want to let her down. Especially now, when there is stuff which his biological cycle won't really appreciate going down either.

'It's okay, Shadab…I know the house is a mess…you could still show me.'

Women. They know men so well. At least, their cleanliness skills.

'Okay I will…but baby, did you have lunch?' he begins to calculate the time difference. 'It must be around 3 p.m. over there.'

His attempt to change the topic is successful.

'Yes, I did…the campus canteen is not all that bad…I mean I could manage…Mom took me to this Indian restaurant yesterday… sex bomb butter chicken…I don't know what I'll do once she leaves tomorrow.'

'Yaaaa!' a large yawn escapes his mouth, not letting him complete.

'It must be very late there…what's the time?' she asks, a little guilty.

'12.03,' he says quickly and tries hard to kill a yawn but it finds an opening. It's been a tiring, long day for him.

'You look tired…go to sleep,' she says.

'No,' he says firmly.

'Shadab…it won't work this way…You'll begin with your college soon and so would I…We have to plan this out…so it doesn't become a burden for us,' she suggests.

'A burden?' he asks, raised eyebrows.

'Parvez…remember how we'd discussed about the *career comes first* policy. Let's just…'

He cuts in.

'I get it…we make schedules. Don't screw our college and studies. Instead screw each other.'

'Yeah,' she says quickly. 'No, I mean not the last clause.'

They both laugh.

'I've got an idea. We both get two wall clocks. Keep one clock according to the Indian time and one according to the time here,' she suggests.

'Brilliant Arnika…why can't I come up with such ideas?' he questions.

'Ha…because you're a guy and you don't want chick flicks…I saw this in a movie.'

They both laugh. Again.

'Arnika…baby…can we do it now…please?' he pleads after a few more minutes of random talk. He's messaged Ritesh in the meanwhile, to know when he'll be back.

'Not soon. Not until I get to unhook,' has been his reply and the very thought that his two best friends are going to or probably are making out by now, has turned him on, all the more…

'Why don't you just watch porn?' she says with a devil's twinkle.

'Why don't we make our own little porno?' he retorts back.

'You do realize the power of technology…I could video record you doing all of this.' Arnika warns him playfully. 'I could earn some money with it too.'

'But that turns me on all the more,' he says adjusting the webcam again towards well...ummm.

'Fine...do whatever you want...but don't forget to watch debonair.com tomorrow,' she says very seriously.

'Arrrnii.'

His breath is heavy. Heavy enough.

The visual is graphic. Graphic enough.

She gives in. No rule book says girls can't get turned on.

The act begins. The maximum she does is play around with her T-shirt. Well, play around exceedingly well with her T-shirt.

Words are exchanged. Subtle. Gentle. Then hurried. Wild. Roles assumed.

'Arnniiii,' Shadab's voice and body are shaking vigorously.

'Shadab,' her tale is no different.

'Arnii,' he repeats.

'Shadabbbb,' it's another call.

'Arniiiiiii,' this time louder. Wilder. Almost there.

His headphones are almost about to explode with all the moaning.

'SHADABBB?' a male voice this time beckons him.

They both freeze. In India. In New York.

'Ritesh...you son of a bitch,' Shadab shouts as he turns around and closes the laptop screen and takes off his headphones and keeps the laptop on a certain risen tent. In the same action breath.

'Ssorry man...I thought you were...I mean...carry on,' he says embarrassed. 'And oh,' he stops at the door again. 'Hi Arnika!' He shouts loud enough for her to hear and rushes out before Shadab can throw the water bottle at him.

He wears the headphones again and opens the laptop screen.

'Hello...Arni,' he begins carefully.

No reply.

'Hello,' he speaks into the mike again.
No reply.
He opens the blinking Skype messenger only to find her offline.

MOM came. Sorry. Will ttyl…ily…bye.

'Great,' Shadab says, looking at his boxers. 'Ritesh,' he gets up from the bed, throwing away his laptop and runs towards his room. There's some screwing to be done. He has no other choice, it seems. This is just the beginning.

fifteen

And what do you do on your first anniversary, if you're not together?
Get drunk...puke...fight...abuse...accuse...decide to break up...
try to outdo each other in verbal tennis...
yet in the end...make good use of the webcams.

12 July 2010

11.45 p.m. (IST)
Three sixty-five days. Eight thousand seven hundred sixty hours. Five lakh twenty-five thousand six hundred minutes. Three crore fifteen lakh thirty-six thousand seconds. That's a lot of maths for the physical compatibility of two chemically bonded carbon-based forms, who have also forged biological relations.

A year together.

Shadab opens the door to his room, darts his shoes aimlessly into the air, attacks his cupboard, strips what he's worn for the day and slips quickly into a black shirt and blue jeans. Her favourite.

Next, he runs out to the kitchen, checking the time on the way. 11.52 p.m. Eight minutes for their anniversary to begin.

They've already planned it out.

12 a.m. Here.

2.30 p.m. There.

She's decided to skip her lecture and rush back to her hostel room. Her mother's left for India. Once she's in her room. Alone. They both come online on Skype.

Video call.

This time not being disturbed by ANYONE. Ritesh has gone clubbing with Alisha and has been specifically instructed to call before entering the house.

Gifts.

An integral part of any celebration, especially if it's a relationship. Technology and his Dad's bank balance have helped. He's arranged for flowers and a gold pendant bearing their names' initials, to be delivered to her through www.giftsforamerica.com.

She's arranged for his gift to be delivered to him during the day. A pair of Gucci shades. She's bought them on eBay. Two months of savings. A handmade card.

Shadab's gone the extra mile to surprise her. Candles in the room. Soft music. Her favourite clothes. A cake. Flowers. Everything adaptable to the webcam, that'll make her feel her presence in his room.

His life!
His heart!

11.58 p.m.
Everything has been arranged. He's staring at the laptop screen, looking at their pictures on Facebook, waiting for her to come online.

11.59 p.m.
He picks up his cell phone and calls her. No answer. A balloon of pain bursts in his stomach. He calls again. No one answers it again. Another call. This time the computer-generated voice informs him that her cell is switched off.

12 a.m.
His eyes are liquid again. Piercing liquid. The candles on the cake, in the room, flicker helplessly. He stares blankly at the laptop screen. Random questions cloud his head.

Is she okay? Why is her phone not reachable? Why did it get switched off all of a sudden?

12.04 a.m.
His mobile comes to life. So do the dying aspirations. He excitedly looks at the screen, only to find 'Ritesh' flashing on it. He disconnects the call.

The candles have begun to melt.

12.07 a.m.
The congratulatory messages begin to pour. The toll of unread messages in his mobile begins to rise. Facebook notifications increase. He doesn't care to reply. Not even to his mother's missed call.

1.15 a.m.
The speakers of his laptop come to life, killing the depressing silence in the room. The patented Skype tone reaches his ears as he gulps

down a large sip from the beer can.

He, deprived of excitement, double clicks on the laptop's mouse pad and answers the call, once his Skype messenger opens. He ignores the video option from his side while hers begins in a few moments.

There she is. Beautiful as ever.

'Hey!!!!!!!!!!' Arnika's voice is brimming with excitement.

'Hi,' he replies after a prolonged pause.

'What's wrong with your webcam? Why can't I see you?' she questions, ignoring the pause, behaving as if nothing wrong has happened.

'Hmmm,' he grunts, 'it's not like you want to see me anyway,' he ends, gulping down another sip from the can. His fourth beer can.

She takes a deep breath before replying. He sees her eyes close momentarily, just as she performs the action and his heart almost melts, by the very sight. Almost. Not. Completely.

'Shadab...baby...I know you're angry and I'm SORRY...Mr Philip...my law lecturer called me in...there were some doubts regarding my submission.'

'K.' K is not a reply. It's a kick in your balls. Just that, she doesn't have any.

There's silence again. He can see dejection creep all over her face, yet the cemented layers of hurt and ego over his heart won't melt.

'Happy anniversary,' her voice is distant.

'Oh yeah...I didn't realize...to you too,' his response is diabolic and instant.

'You know what...that's it!!' her patience is murdered too.

'THAT'S IT!!! THAT'S IT! You know what...that's not it...I HAVE BEEN WAITING FOR A BLOODY HOUR...LIKE AN ARSE...ALL DRESSED UP,' he pauses, turns on his webcam and continues, 'with the candles, cake...and you want is to attend some lame class...cause, why would you care? You never have... It's always been me...,' hot tears well up in his eyes and he brushes them away, continuing, 'you, bloody don't love me Arnika...all you, bloody, love is...' he pauses.

Words in an argument are like a thick soup. The colder they get, the more difficult it is for them to get digested.

'You've been drinking,' she says, after she looks at his bloodshot eyes and the beer can, in the view the webcam is giving.

He gives a silent reply.

'Just get lost,' she slurs. Booze is a bummer. Anytime.

'Fine...call me when you care,' he snaps.

'Call me when you're sober.'

'I'll call you after I get laid.'

'Yes...that's what you want anyway...you don't love me... You have a dick in place of your heart.'

'You know better where what is.'

'You know what... I've had enough of you... Go enjoy your life... Get laid, do it with anything that has a hole... bye.'

She's about to hang up when he begins, 'Okay...cut the call... go away...but remember...twenty years hence, one night when you've hit menopause and your fat husband is busy shagging in the washroom as you sit alone on your king-sized bed, secretly searching cosmo for answers to your sagging breasts and unsatisfied urges...you'll remember me and you'd be like why did I fight with Shadab on our first anniversary,' he blurts it all, in one go.

Awkward silence. Both ends. Rhythmic, heavy breaths. Both ends. Intent eyes, both ends.

And then her jaw relaxes into a smile. A year is strong enough for the shittiest of fights to get flushed down the drain and pave way for new, Harpic-clean moments. Just like the one that follows next.

'I don't want this to end Shadab...you know it...I know it...I love you,' she says softly.

'Arni...,' emotions wrestle with his vocals. 'Arni...I love you too,' his vocals finally win.

'Promise me...you won't ever leave me,' she's at her emotional best.

'I promise,' he says with all the seriousness he can muster 'but...'

'But?' she asks confused.

'But...I...just...need...to...,' he lurches his head forward in a jerk.

'Are you okay?' Arnika questions, concerned.

'Mee...yeah...no,' he takes off his headphones and dashes towards his washroom.

BWAEEEEEEEE...she hears him choke, faintly in the background.

Four beers can fuck any empty stomach.

He returns after a few minutes, wiping his face with a towel.

'Yessss,' she hears and sees him as he comes back in the webcam view, headphone's placed around his ears again.

'Too much to handle?'

She serves the ball in his court.

Fifteen. Love.

'Gives me company...when someone is busy with her law professor.'

Her next serve is answered well.

Fifteen. Fifteen.

'Correction...sexy law professor.'

This time, she smashes the ball, taking him by total surprise.

Thirty. Fifteen.

'Okay...stop...I don't want to fight again...but still, just for

General knowledge... how old is the professor?'

Forty. Fifteen.

'Age is just a number.'

And she wants to win by a large margin... it seems.

'You got that right, Arni,' the webcam's angle is inappropriately shifted again. 'Age is just a number... what matters is what lies within.'

He's made an ace of a comeback.

Forty. Thirty.

'YOU ARE SO INAPPROPRIATE.'

Another faulty service.

Forty. Thirty.

'Somebody told me... two nights ago... strangely... that very person ended up being as sarcastic as me... funny isn't it?"

And he's smashed the next serve.

Forty. Forty.

Duece

'Well, like this?' The graphic from her side steams up again.

Advantage! Not fair, she's using techniques way beyond tennis.

'Certainly,' it's easier for him to take his shirt off.

GAME OVER. *She wins. He loses. But does he?*

sixteen

And then 'life' happens to their relationship...

July 2010—December 2010

July

God bless the berry. Amen.

If Apple was the fruit of the century for Adam and Eve, Blackberry is the fruit of the century for Shadab and Arnika.

Ever since she's got herself a local number and her BBM services have been activated, all they've done is to message each other. ALL THE TIME. Like, seriously, all the time.

Texts at the speed of fast humping.

Day here, night there. Night here, day there, in college, classroom or canteen. Washroom or try room, they've texted each other. Frivolous random texts, as random as Shadab telling Arnika at 4 a.m. in the night about how bad his fart smells or Arnika pinging him, while he's in class, just to let him know, she's down. The randomness does not end here.

Every day, after her classes get over, she makes it a point to call him. For two minutes or twenty, she's always heard his voice. It's like calcium to her bones.

Every night, whether at home, in boxers or at a club, in his most crisp shirt, he makes it a point to talk to her. Yes, he talks to her, even if he's sloshed deep neck in beer.

They're resolute about it. Even more particular than Simi Grewal is about her whites. That she looks like a divine beauty in it is a separate story.

Pictures as unnecessary as condoms in a monastery.

She goes shopping. Every girl does. She tries a multitude of odd dresses, shoes, scans a truckful of bags. Every girl does. Spoiled by choice, she ends confused on what to buy. She's a girl after all. She finds a quick solution. Yes, she's a girl for sure. She takes out her Blackberry and clicks away to glory, only to send all the pictures to Shadab. Well, there's nothing wrong with taking your boyfriend's opinion on a one-piece, he'll be honestly interested only to take off, if he was not seven seas apart, but not at the expense of his sleep. Especially after he's had this really tiring day at college and is nine beers down.

Still he replies.

Randomly choosing the brightest picture as the best. It hurts his eye the most. He has no choice. As of now. At least.

It's just a matter of time.

7.45 p.m. (IST)

24 July 2010

'Wow...can you believe these...onions are forty-five rupees a kg?' Ritesh says to Shadab as they pass the vegetable section in the supermarket, located on the nearby acre of their apartment.

Yes, they've come grocery shopping. Staying alone makes you do such stuff.

'Yes Mom...I know,' Shadab replies back as they laugh, dragging the shopping cart, juggling with the list Alisha has helped them prepare.

Feminine touch is divine. Be it any matter, below the belt or buying groceries.

'Okay...I think, we're almost done here,' Ritesh comments, scanning the mountain of commodities in their shopping cart. 'You sure...we aren't forgetting anything?' he adds, a little doubtful.

Both the guys. Typical of being ball-bearers, scratch their chins and think.

'Condoms!' Ritesh exclaims.

'Coffee!' Shadab exclaims!

Both necessities.

Different people.

Different uses.

Different reasons.

Ritesh, getting to meet Alisha, even more than when they were in Chandigarh, aptly walks off the counter housing contraceptives while Shadab, screwed by longitudes and latitudes, as an illegitimate child of different time zones, walks up to the rack, where coffee jars are kept.

Five packets of condoms are bought that day to fund Ritesh's hormonal needs.

Five jars of coffee are also bought to fund Shadab's nocturnal deeds.

Coffee. Black. Low sugar, helps Shadab kill the sleep willingly and his taste buds unwillingly, after a long day at college, for an even longer night by the laptop with Arnika. He's hardly used his bed for the last few nights. To sleep that is.

It's just a matter of time. Pun intended.

The faint dark circles are just an added bonus to this long-distance package yet he doesn't give an iota of fuck to it. Dark circles can be concealed for his theatre performances and another fifteen minutes with Arnika are a bumper bargain against an hour less of sleeping.

At least, that's what he thinks. For now. Just for now. Maybe.

August

I'm sorry...I am committed...

8 August 2010

College is like a fishing pond with all types of catch. Yet. There are some vegetarian fishermen around. Those who know they have it in them to catch a meal but prefer to eat at home. Every day. Even on the weekends. Sadly.

Nobody in this world would endorse this statement with such ball-blasting enthusiasm as Shadab does. College indeed is a pond full of fish. But he's turned vegetarian. For Arnika's sake.

Chicks struggling to become hens. With shorts, seeming to be sponsored by bikini-manufacturing companies; skirts, long enough by courtesy, divulging more than they intend to hide.

It's not easy to turn a blind eye to all of this and more. Not when you're considered hot and approached often through random chats, in the canteen, in the class, in the amphitheatre, which inevitably end at a 'coffee ask out' or a request for number exchange.

It's like being rock hard, yet not being able to cum. Sheer, pure frustration.

Sample this...

The college canteen. One random morning. He's bunked his English literature lecture. It's an old habit. He's not the only one though.

'Hi... are you connected? I really need to send this e-mail.'

Shadab stops typing an e-mail that he's writing to Arnika on his laptop and looks up only to find Aastha, his hot classmate with the firmest butt ever, standing expectantly next to the lone empty chair.

It's time for a reply and Shadab duly complies with a 'Yup.'

'Umm... Is anyone seated here?' she asks, getting ready to pull the unoccupied chair.

'No... wait!' Shadab begins and she freezes midway.

Awkward moment for both of them.

Arnika's face has flashed in front of his eyes. Momentarily. That's what happens when you feed your conscience with honesty and loyalty.

He brushes it away and begins, 'My... my imaginary friend from Narnia... Mr Rhino's been soaking in all the Vitamin D here... don't want it to be all that thorny for you.' He gets up and continues, 'C'mon Mr Rhino... be a gentleman and let the beautiful lady sit,' he ends, pulling the chair for her.

It's the best flirt she's encountered till now, in her entire, countlessly approached, by all types of guys, life. She thinks. It's the best cover up he's ever thought of. He thinks.

'Thank you, Mr Rhino,' she tilts her head, smiles the 'twinkle-in-the-eye' smile and sits.

Shadab quickly walks back to his seat and sits down. He can't help but take his eyes down the valley. The brown. Chocolate valley.

'So...can I have your lap...,' a message on her mobile cuts her request shot.

'My lap?' he exclaims, still stealing guilty looks.

'Top,' she adds and smiles, still replying to the SMS on her cell, using her fingers at a speed men won't mind getting castrated for. Actually in retrospect, they would. 'Yes,' she finishes texting and looks at him, in his eyes. 'Can I have it now?'

Dude. Is she hot! Merger with it, the fact that she's been subtly flashing him smiles ever since he's helped her reverse her car in the college parking a week ago.

'The laptop...here,' he murmurs softly and looks down at the screen.

Arnika and his picture. The wallpaper of his homepage. He flushes out all the nasty thoughts that have cropped in his pot of a mind in the last few minutes. It pays to be loyal. It pays a lot. Ask him. Ask what's conspiring down under. He passes the laptop.

Aastha's smile goes into a cardiac arrest on seeing his homepage wallpaper. Shadab and Arnika's picture. Hugging each other. Just like a couple.

Sexy. Subtle. Visibly rich. Aastha had already zeroed in on him. For the next few weeks at least she's disappointed.

'Oh...I didn't know you were already taken,' she says, bending a little to apparently adjust her sandal. The fact the she's wearing a tube top isn't helping his case.

'Yup...been more than a year,' he says with a pride toddlers often exhibit over their toys.

'Wow that's sweet...so... Is she here in Delhi?'

The urgent e-mail she had to send is forgotten about. Only if there was an e-mail to be sent, in the first place.

'No...New York.'

'WOW...that is some distance even for a LDR,' she says, blowing some air over her over-manicured nails.

'Well...she's too good to let go off,' he says with dreamy eyes.

'That I can see...she's pretty.' *'Bitch,'* she says internally.

'I know.'

'You know what, I was in a LDR myself. It didn't work out though. I'm better off being single,' she turns pensive for a moment. Just for a moment. 'But, it always good to know that at least somebody believes in love.'

He smiles. She does too.

After a few minutes of animated conversations, more smiles happen.

Another ten minutes pass. A lot of smiles are exchanged. There is chemistry for sure.

She's telling him about how this guy in their class hit upon her, when Shadab suddenly brings his hand close to his ear, encircles it, acting as if he's listening to someone. 'Mr Rhino wants to know... if you like cold coffee or coke?'

There is laughter. This time. Genuine laughter. Laughter that makes her want him all the more. Laughter that makes him want her all the more.

As a friend.

Maybe. As of now. At least.

A shoulder to sleep on. Not his shoulder though.

24 August 2010

'Hey Arnika...we're about to reach, get up,' Jason, her classmate and new-found friend, shakes her a little as she refuses to lift her head from his shoulder.

They are travelling to the academic block from the residential buildings, in the college bus, for their first lecture. Their first lecture at 8 a.m. and if that wasn't enough, it's a Monday.

'No sha...I don't...get...up,' Arnika mutters, restricting half the words to her mouth and refusing to open her eyes. She snuggles on to Jason's chest, a little more.

He doesn't mind it. Which normal boy with balls full of zap would?

Last night had been tough for her. Shadab had had a major argument with his Dad and she had to submit a fifteen hundred words paper of law and equity, this morning.

Both needed her attention. Hundred per cent attention.

Yet.

She'd chosen love over law.

They'd fought on their first anniversary for the same reason. Repeated mistakes are called habits and she didn't want this to become one.

Sleep had happened only at 3.30 a.m. Sunrise at 6 a.m. and she'd opened her eyes again at seven, just after the dog of a clock had started to bark.

'I lo...u...Sha...dab,' she murmurs in her trance as Jason combs a few astray strands of her hair.

She's dreaming of Shadab being there with her. When she goes sightseeing. When she goes to this coffee shop which rapes

Cappuccino like no one else can. When she goes clubbing with her new-found friends. When she sits under the huge banyan tree, in the university premises. She dreams of his shoulder and her head resting on it.

And as an involuntary response, her hand reaches out to encircle Jason's hand. He willingly gives her the support.

Shadab, he's seen the guy on her Facebook profile. He knows, they are thick. He also knows, distance can break the strongest of bonds. His hands clasp hers softly.

Suddenly her eyes open and she gets up in a flash. Maybe it's the unfamiliarity of his touch. Maybe it's the erection he's got in the past few minutes and she can feel it.

'I am so sorry,' she says, embarrassed, looking away from Jason.

'Don't be...I didn't mind any of it,' he replies back.

'But I did,' she whispers to herself, looking out of the glass window.

The distance is getting to her.

Maybe. As of now. At least.

September

Fight. Fight. Fight.
24 September 2010

1.30 a.m. (IST)
4 p.m. (EST)

'So...Aastha...seems to be a nice girl. You both look cute in her display picture on Facebook...where is this?' Is Arnika's first comment-cum-question, after the customary salutations have been exchanged, that night in India, day in New York, as they both sit on their respective beds and video call through Skype.

'We all went clubbing last weekend...Hype...told yeah... remember...,' he replies confidentially. There's nothing for him to hide. At least till now.

'Hype?...Oh, yes...I remember...when I'd called you at around 4 a.m. your time and you were so drunk, you were asking me if I was single and would like to go out for coffee...' He begins to laugh before she can complete.

'I was just fooling around Arni...swear on my balls,' he raises one hand, knots the fingers of his other into a small cross over his neck.

'Yeah...yeah...I believe you,' her mobile begins to ring and she fishes it out of her shorts' pocket and takes the call.

'Hey J,' she chirps and its echo rebounds hard in his ears.

'Okay...wait...I think I have it,' she says, getting up and going away from the webcam's view, leaving him with her stale sperm-coloured wall to see.

The video call hasn't been paused or cut. The microphone hasn't been switched off. Shadab can hear her faint voice, echoing in the room.

J. Who the fuck is J? What kind of a name is J? Trust these Americans to come out with the most weird names but still, J? Arnika's never told him anything about J. Is it a code word? Is it a signal? Why is she laughing? Have they shared a cheap, personal joke? He thinks. He pushes his headphones into his ears, spanking them with his hands, trying to make sense of the soft voices he can hear in the background.

'Yes, I know...,' he deciphers her say. 'Stop now...I'll die,' another voice syllable is deciphered by him in the next few seconds.

'Okay...thank you Jason...you're a sweetheart,' her voice strangely becomes clearer with each passing second and suddenly she comes and sits back on the bed. Without the mobile stuck to her ear.

'YOU WERE EAVSDROPPING ON ME, SHADAB PARVEZ!' She accuses him as she puts on her headphones.

'Me? No...no!' his head is lurched forward. His hands still stuck to his headphones. His expressions. All Sherlock Holmes. It's rather too easy to guess, especially for a girl.

No wonder, actions speak louder than words.

'Admit it, princess...I could see you from my table, even if you couldn't and you were trying to know what's happening,' she says with buckled conviction.

'Okay...maybe I was,' he changes his position and lies down on the bed.

Shadab's known about Jason. He's searched all about him ever since she added him on Facebook. Precisely three weeks and four days back.

He has her password.

Just like Arnika has his.

The very same way she's seen Aastha's profile pictures with such clarity.

Helps keep a tab on each other. Mutual trust. It's like their joint account in a bank, the amount increasing every day.

So, coming back to Jason.

A friend she's made in college. He lives near her hostel. They have quite a few subjects in common, to study that is. They are normal friends. Healthy friends. Coffee friends. DAMN!

'So when did Jason become J?' His 'put up' indifferent tone doesn't work with her. She knows him inside out. Literally.

'Since we ended up kissing last weekend in his room,' comes

the reply.

'Ha ha... funny,' he makes no intention to hide his displeasure.

'Awww... is my princess jealous?' she teases.

'Go away,' he says like a girl and keeps a hand over the webcam of his laptop. Not letting her see him.

Role reversal. That's how it goes in their relationship. Shadab, the damsel in distress, the princess. Arnika, the hunk, the horse-humping prince.

'Seriously, princess,' she groans, 'do I ever get suspicious about Aastha even if you're out, drunk as a pig with her at 4 a.m. on weekends?' She's assumed that they were still together; sadly, her assumption is foolproof.

He removes his finger from the webcam lens and begins. Again getting up to sit.

'Who on the face of fuck said I was getting suspicious?'

'Errr...you...your voice...your tone...your actions...you're getting so narrow minded.'

'Oh yea?' he stretches his hand and breaks his knuckles. 'So I'm narrow minded...who lets you go out whenever you want with anybody you like, wearing whatever you want...anytime you like?'

Blame it on the mosquitoes in Delhi. Blame it on the plumber who's not come to repair the flush of his toilet. Blame it on a pimple that has decided to camp on his forehead. Blame it on the sticky Maggi he's had for dinner. Blame it on Mallu porn that he's accidentally downloaded from torrents. It's almost a fight.

His veins are leaking hot, boiling blood.

She wets her lips with her tongue. Prepared for any battle. *Sheesh*, that sounds perverted.

'I can't believe you have a problem with what I wear... I wear the same clothes I used to wear when I was with you. Why didn't you have a problem back then?' she counter questions.

What she wears wasn't exactly even the topic of discussion. Okay, topic of aggressive disagreement. But that's the beauty of a fight—it's origin is as fickle as a prostitute's virginity.

'Because back then, you were with me...not in a horny country like America...alone...careless...but why would you care?' he counter questions the counter-questioned question.

'Exactly, why would I care? I don't care about anything Shadab...not you...not Ma...not even us...that's why I'm stupid enough to make sure I talk to you even if I have abandoned my plans just for your happiness but it's not like you care...Do you?'

YOUR HAPPINESS. Singular phrase. It stings him. The venom reacts pretty fast.

'My happiness? I've stayed up till so late for the past two months, I can guess the changing security guards by their voices and you think it's about my happiness and not yours?'

Then he does just what he shouldn't. The clouds fart. The winds burp. The windows bang.

HE POINTS A FINGER AT HER. A MERE SELFLESS FINGER.

Fight origin changed yet again.

'How dare you point a finger at me?' she counter questions the already countered-questioned question.

'I...I...I...I felt like doing it,' he stutters. This isn't what they were fighting about. He thinks internally. FOUL!

'Fine...you know what...call me when you think you can keep your fingers in control.'

'You've spoiled my fingers...they were always in control before you and your desires came into the scene.'

Silence. She can't believe he just said that. He can't believe it too.

'Bye,' she says and cuts the call. She goes offline in the next second and switches off her mobile in the second that follows.

Not that he tries to call her anyway.

It's their first fight.

Their only fight.

As of now. At least.

And there's water...from the clouds...from the eyes...

26 September 2010

Rain. The soft showers, the cold breeze, the tingling music of the droplets. The failure of the drainage system. The roads leaking, puking like they've had neat Vodka and forgotten the lemons. The colourful umbrellas. The heads which collide behind them. Rain. The car mirrors which get fogged simply by mere verbal interactions. The clothes deciding to commit themselves to the body. The B looking like a D. The hands squeezing everything that's round. Rain. Couples everywhere. Hand in hand. Arm in arm. That in that. The birds. Chirping like they've decided to go for a mammoth gang-bang!

'It's raining and I feel lonely. I miss you.'

Shadab updates this as his Facebook status as he sits by the window, stretched legs, laptop heating his crotch and the wind spraying a few raindrops on his face.

He's skipped college today. The weather, the fight, make him feel like he's on periods. Down, irritated and gloomy. He reaches for his mobile and begins to dial Arnika's number, only to cut the call, even before it's made.

Heard of ego? It stinks.

He dials her number again, simultaneously opening her Facebook profile. Her last update has been four hours ago. He checks the time on his laptop clock. It's been set according to the time in New York.

3 a.m.

It's been more than twenty-four hours. They've not exchanged a word. His mouth turns dry at the very thought.

He sends a text to Ritesh next. The reply comes in no time.

In class. Call you in fifteen minutes.

Exasperated.

He again dials a number.

This call is answered in nanoseconds.

'Hey...lo...what is up?'

'Nothing...just got up...you say.'

'Nothing.'

'You don't sound too good to me? The fight's still on?'

'Yes. Where are you?'

'Standing at the college bus stop. Strange how it rains just the day I don't get my car...anyway...why didn't you come today? You do know, your attendance is lower than our psychology teacher's IQ.'

A smile crops up on his face. His first smile after the fight. Arnika isn't the cause though.

'Aastha...are you free right now?'

'Only if it's hot cappuccino at Costa.'

Another smile.

'I'll be there in fifteen.'

The call is cut. He's feeling better. Lighter. Though, she's still there at the back of his mind.

At least for now. Maybe. That is.

October

Re-solve.

3 October 2010

Those three magical words. They make the world go round. And round. And round. And round. Those three magical words. The essence of any relationship. Those three magical words. They sprinkle freshness into the most grim situations. Those three magical words. They bind. Sometimes way too closely. Those three magical words. The glory of sunrise. The romanticism of moonlight. Those three magical words. It takes bush-cricket testicles to mutter them. It takes multilayered foundation capacity to absorb them.

Those three magical words. They end every fight. Dilute every misunderstanding. Clear every misconception. Kill all the arguments. Bring smiles. Satiate the ego pangs.

Those three magical words.

'I WAS WRONG!'

Arnika finally texts Shadab, ending their week-long fight.

Her pillow is tired of being wet. His lungs, tired of handling all the smoke. For the last six days. And nights.

Yes. One week. Seven days. And nights? Yes nights.

No talking. No texting. Not even a single, lonely, poor, destitute message.

Three magical words are ushered from his side in reply.

'I AM SORRY!'

Her eyes twinkle on reading the reply. Rats getting high on

Italian cheese. That's just the emotion.

And then finally the call is made. A thousand sentences exchanged. A hundred emotions felt. And in the end, the three magical words are said again to each other.

I LOVE YOU.

As of now. Maybe that is.

November

S__P__A__C__E

11 November 2010

All good things come to an end. It's how Nature scores and we mortals get laid. Left. Right. Centre.

Holidays finish. Orgasms exhaust. Smiles vanish. Chocolates melt. Tandoori chicken burn. All good things come to this sad end. Paving way for bad things to happen. Things as irritating as an unnecessary early morning hard on. A *mithia*-fed pimple on the nose. An allergy on the butt. A fight with your boyfriend. Again.

Blackberry Messenger Chat.

12.30 p.m. (IST)

3.30 a.m. (EST)
He pings her. Messages next.
There?

Five minutes go by. No reply. He pings her again. No reply again. He calls her. Anger burned, beer-hit eyes. Last night's hangover is still seducing him as he sits in his car outside his college. He was in the college auditorium, practising with the college theatre group for their fest performance some time ago. All was well. Except for the hangover headache. Then somebody asked someone to YouTube a video and his laptop was spotted. Forced by habit, he'd opened her profile on Facebook as the video had streamed. AND THEN. He'd seen something which had pissed him to the core. He'd excused himself and rushed out to his car.

Another message. Another ping. No reply.

He calls her up. No reply. The anger's reached its peak. He needs a cigarette. He lights his third when he calls her for the twelfth time. Yet, no reply. A minor streak of worry diffuses his anger.

In frustration he throws his cell on the passenger seat and lights the last cigarette, he has in his pocket. He doesn't keep a pack now. Arnika's instructions. He's trying to quit. For her sake. For their sake.

He's on his last drag when his cell beeps. The enthusiasm of her reply is quickly replaced by the worry of Ankush, his group member's message. Everybody is waiting inside. He's playing one of the principal characters. They need to practise.

He asks for ten more minutes in reply and tries calling her for the one last time. Nobody answers. Again. As a final resort, he dials her friend and dorm neighbour, Taashi's number.

He begins as soon as the call is answered, on the first try itself.

'Hey Taashi... I'm so sorry for calling so late but can you walk over to Arnika's room and check if everything is okay... she's not answering my calls...'

'Shadab?'

'Hello... Arnika?... Is that you?' There's loud music in the background. Trance music. It simply implies two things. There's a party and it has booze.

'Hi baby...is everything okay?' she shouts, trying to outdo the music as she climbs a flight of stairs and walks out to the balcony. Her tone is too chirpy. Like she's some beers down or high on candy.

'Where are you? Why aren't you taking my calls? Where is this noise coming from?'

Questions. Questions.

She answers them all.

'I'm at a dorm party and I forgot my cell in my room. What's up? Aren't you in college?'

Visual. Graphic pictures of the party flash before him. He's seen American Pie. All of them.

'WHAT ARE YOU DOING OUT SO LATE?' the volcano erupts. There's mild background music too.

She's confused. A few tequila shots are bound to numb your senses. Just by a little margin.

'Why are you shouting at me?'

'Who's this guy Arjun? What's with the picture he's tagged you in your Facebook profile? Why are you sitting in his lap?'

'Arjun lived across my dorm room and had met at one of those inconsequential dorm parties that didn't matter but as time flew, he started to matter. In all healthy connotations. Sweet guy. Funny. Almost like a new best friend in an alien city.'

The main reason for him calling her.

Silence.

She's chosen to remain that way. All he can hear is his own heavy breathing. And the 'call waiting' beeps from someone inside.

'Arnika...I know you're there,' he coughs. 'Answer me.'

'Been smoking?' she hisses.

'Don't change the topic,' he fights back.

She takes a deep breath.

'Listen... I'll call you tomorrow, okay? I don't want to spoil my mood right now.'

'NO! Answer me.'

'Listen, we'll talk when you're not so hyper.'

'Fuck you, Arnika. You're the one who's clicking pictures with random guys. You're the one who's out at some guy's place and I am getting hyper?'

'You're out every weekend! I don't fuck about it. What is your problem? Can't I have a life?'

'Without me...you cannot.'

'Huh...'

'Hey Arni...what are you doing outside? I've been looking for you all over.'

An accented male voice is heard in the background. It fucks his mind all the more.

'I'll be back Arjun...give me two minutes.'

She doesn't even think of covering the receiver with her hand. He should know. He better should know. Back on the call.

'Yes Shadab...anything else you want to say?'

'No. Nothing at all. Don't let me stop you. Arjun is waiting,' he's at his sarcastic best.

'Okay...I'll talk to you later then...and oh yes, for the record, you're my boyfriend and not my father. So you don't really have to tell me if I can get drunk at four in the night or not.'

He laughs. An artificial. Mean. Evil. Laugh.

'I wish I didn't have to be your father most of the times.'

Words kill. He's an assassin.

Her voice breaks. There's water in the eyes.

'I'll remember.'

She tastes salt.

He...well, nothing but rage. Blind rage.

The call is cut.

It's a difficult phase for them. But, it will pass. At least for now. Perhaps. Maybe. That is.

It's official: It's complicated.

13 November 2010

Hey Princess,

So how are you? How's the play coming up? How's Ritesh and Al? Ummmm...Shadab...Okay listen, let's just not make this any shittier than it already is.

Princess, I love you. Yes, despite you being you, I seriously do. And balls to everything that happened that day. More of night actually.

It kills to not kiss you every time the moon's acting so girly and gay. It kills to know you won't be there when I feel like getting pig drunk. It kills to go clubbing without you. Agreed, you get offered free drinks all the time and that too shit expensive ones! Okay I'm going a little off track here... Yes, so, it kills to not blow my nose into your shirt when I'm watching all the movies you hated :D. Also there's nobody to irritate or make a sandwich for.

Princess, the last few months have been challenging to say the least. We've laughed, cried, had online dates, done all that we shouldn't have on Skype. We've argued on the most trivial matters. God, it almost feels like we're married. Except you know what part of it.

I've missed you. I've missed us. You're the best thing that has happened in my life. You and my new Louis Vuitton bag actually :P

Princess, what's wrong? Why are we fighting every second week? It's not helping me or my grades. I know it's affecting your performance and it's definitely not what WE want.

So Shadab, you might consider me the biggest bitch in the history of bitchkind by the end of it all, but I've decided that we need to give 'US' some rest. I know you must be frowning by now, thinking this is again one of my 'let her blab moments', but this time I'm serious.

He can't decide whether to continue to frown or smile. She knows him so well and he bloody knows that as well.

No, we aren't breaking up. No, not even if you want it to. You're a rich guy, I won't let you go so easily. This is more of a cooling off period. It's time we decided to give SHADAB and ARNIKA some time. To think of it, for the past few months we've been cursing the lives we always wanted to lead. This time won't return, Shadab, nor would you or I get the opportunity to chase our ambitions. Moreover, if I get to become an ambassador, we'd get to travel business class free. Sexy, right?

So, here's the plan. WE DON'T CALL, TEXT MESSAGE, PING each other till I come back next month. It'll make us stronger. Help us prioritize, make us realize what we want and what we have.

You might just hate me for this. Making it complicated. You might just want to dump me or cheat on me which is

> *perfectly all right because I can't ruin you or your life for what I feel is right. Stop dialling my number and continue reading the mail.*

His fingers freeze on his cell's keypad.

> *I mean it this time. Don't worry, I won't come back empty handed. You'll get your gifts. It's just a month and some days.*
>
> *I'm blocking you from my Facebook account till I'm back. I think it'll help.*
>
> *I hope you know, I mean good for you, for me, for us. And yes, I've been talking to aunty all this while. Call her more often. She really misses you.*
>
> *I love you… I guess.*
>
> *Your humping prince*
>
> *And I almost forgot to tell you. Arjun's gay. So the lap. It's more of a sister thing. I love you.*

After-effects.

14 November 2010

He calls her. Every hour. Repeatedly. He pings her. He messages her. Till his fingers ache.

In the evening, she deletes him from BBM too.

He cries. Till his eyes burn.

He smokes. Till he coughs.

That night, he finally logs on to Facebook and changes his relationship status.

'It's complicated.'

6 December 2010

Alisha, Ritesh, Bani and the old friends try at their own levels to get them back together. Sometimes calling them and putting them in a conference call. Coincidentally, of course.

Sometimes talking to them individually.

But today, they've given up. Nothing would change what's happening. They've realized. Shadab has no time to think about anything. The preparations for the inter-college theatre festival are in full swing. The first one to reach and the last one to leave practice. He's tried hard to stay busy with the play.

The only irony. Their college team is presenting *Romeo and Juliet*.

Arnika's loving it, unapologetically. No one to answer. No one to please.

17 December 2010

'Cheerssss.'

Shadab clanks his beer bottle with the others and gulps down a large sip. They've won. Second position, out of twenty-three colleges. The price money is being put to good use. The call's already been made to Dominos. Beer cans by the dozens already stacked in the fridge.

Ronil, Dhruv, Kabir, Vihaan, Saisha, Pooja, Shivika, Stuti and Ankush. The entire theatre gang. Aastha, Alisha and Ritesh. All the other important people in his life. Everybody's around. Everybody is celebrating. Everybody is laughing. Even Shadab.

He's improving. The decision has been, on an introspective note, positive for him.

Hours pass. Pizza boxes get lighter. Beer bottles cry empty.

People begin to leave. Some on their own, some in the washroom, near the bed, on it, pushed all along to the entrance and then carried by others.

Alisha and Ritesh are the last people to leave, leaving an empty, dirty house and Shadab and Aastha behind. Alone. At two in the night. Just when both are high enough to mistake a toothbrush with a vibrator.

Thirty more minutes elapse. Thirty minutes in which Shadab has silently stacked all the empty beer bottles in one corner. Thirty minutes in which Aastha, though a little tipsy with all the booze, has managed to clean the living room and take everything to the kitchen. Thirty silent minutes in which Shadab, being naturally pretty high, has got struck by a memory rush. Of Arnika.

'Wow…that was some party!' Aastha returns from the kitchen and crashes on to the sofa.

Shadab and two beers join her.

They both take a deep sip. From their own bottles.

'Thinking about something?' she questions, looking directly into his eyes.

'Arnika,' he murmurs instantly.

Another sip is taken.

'Hmmm…does she care for you?'

'What do you mean?' he keeps the bottle on the floor and asks.

'Does she…' she inches her leg forward, making it softly touch his, 'care for you?'

'Obviously she does,' he argues.

'As much as I do?' her voice is faint. Very faint.

He looks into her eyes. She looks back into his. He feels his senses going into a coma, his heart sprinting, his breath getting heavy.

Beer. Hormone. Loneliness. Blame it on any and everything.

Their lips meet. Apart from the other things.

They make out. Like never before.

19 December 2010

6 p.m. (IST)

Ding dong! He rings the doorbell of her house. After six months. Six painfully long months. Arnika's old neighbour, the same who used to disturb every morning, flashes Shadab a smile from his rooftop, as he waits patiently in the porch.

He runs his hand over the hickey Aastha has left him. Guilt can be such a bitch.

An accident. That's what they concluded to call it last morning, once they both got up in the same bed. Without clothes. An accident. They've decided to forget it. Not let it affect their friendship.

The door opens after a few seconds.

'Shadabbb...you've become so thin!' her mother exclaims in his welcome and he bends down to touch her feet. 'Spare the formalities...give me a hug!'

The hug is exchanged. Her mother's fragrance reminds him of her. Real bad. The guilt pang accompanies him as he is ushered to her house's living room next.

Will he tell her? Will she forgive him? Will she also consider it as a drunk accident? He's thought about all the questions. Just the questions.

'What will you have?' her mother, because of being one, asks, breaking his pool of thoughts.

'Nothing aunty...I'm stuffed.'

He genuinely means it. There's nothing like home-cooked food and he's been reinitiating the statement ever since he has returned to Chandigarh for his winter break. Arnika comes back tomorrow for hers as well.

He needs to let her know. Maybe.

Her mother excuses herself and walks away to the kitchen, leaving him alone.

A quick scan around and the wind of memories unzip him to give him a dirty blowjob.

The stairs. One bright evening in October, Arnika snuggling up to him, despite her mother being in her room. The thrill of sitting there. Stuck to each other. *Just like he must have been with Aastha, he shrugs at the afterthought.*

The dining table. Him being taught Economics on a chilly December day. *Economics, that's Aastha's favourite subject too. STOP. He instructs himself.*

The kitchen. The couch outside her grandmother's room where they made out for they couldn't wait to go till her room and she did not want to corrupt her grandmother's room.

The wall painting they'd made together. Still hanging. The family picture he'd complained of not being in it. Everything.

'So...Shadab, tell me...What all plays did I miss?'

Her mother questions, walking back to him with a tray bearing two coke glasses. He gets up and takes the tray from her midway. They both come back and get seated.

'Where's Nani?'

'She's sleeping. I forgot to inform her that you were coming.'

'That's okay, aunty. I'll meet her later,' he takes a sip and adds, 'so what time do I reach the airport tomorrow?'

The calm on her face transforms immediately into concern.

'Arnika...she told me everything...she had called yesterday,' she inches forward and places her hand on his shoulder 'Beta...I'm her mother...I know what's in her mind. She really likes you... but,' she pauses and looks away 'Arnika's seen her Dad walk away on us. She...she believes that love is meant to give you happiness and the day it stops doing that...it...'

There's silence. Silent silence.

'It's a rough patch...that's all,' he murmurs, mostly to comfort himself. *What happened with Aastha was a mistake. And mistakes aren't meant to be repeated.*

'Shadab...I never had a problem when I came to know about you both...because I'd known that you both were passionate individuals and you wouldn't have let this affect your studies... your life...but...'

His face loses all colour. He's heard the same lines. At his home. Mother-to-mother talk. Dangerous.

She begins again, 'I think you should just concentrate on your studies right now.'

'I've already told Mom what I intend to do, aunty...and I'm sure you know that as well,' he gets up to leave.

'Thank you. I won't come to the airport then...ask Arni to give me a call,' he walks to the main door, opens and then closes it. With a bang.

seventeen

And then they meet only to lose them and find themselves…

20 December 2010

6 p.m.

'Watch your tongue.' Whoever coined the phrase did it with much reason. The tongue is such a risky little muscle. It wriggles, slips, pokes and says all that it shouldn't. Shadab knows this so well, especially after what his little muscle had done the previous day.

It's been four hours since Bani called and told him that Arnika's flight has landed. Four hours since they have been breathing the same air. Four hours since he's been glued to his cell, waiting for her call.

Exasperated, killing the little ego left in him, he decides to dial her number. Like an act of *karma*, his phone screen starts blinking, indicating a message from her, as soon as he dials the first digit of her number.

Get dressed. Pick me up in ten. Don't wear your SpongeBob boxers.

He leaves immediately. Ten exact minutes later, he's waiting outside her house. Just like old times. In an attempt to set his hair, he accidentally runs his hand over the little mark of the 'accident' on his neck and a sudden cloud of guilt engulfs him as he adjusts his shirt so that the hickey isn't visible.

Fogged by thoughts, he doesn't even realize when the main

door of her house is opened or when she opens the main gate and walks to his car and open the door.

'Shadab?'

A fairly accented yet totally familiar voice falls on his ears like sunshine and clears all the clouds surrounding him.

'Ar...ni...ka' he turns and gasps. The day is here after all these months.

She jumps inside the car and hugs him the next instant, the car door closing behind on its own.

Shadab reciprocates the passion. 'I've missed you so much, baby,' he hisses in her ear, her hair strands stuck to his lips. 'I've missed you so much.' he continues, driving his hand over her back, trying to cover every inch of it. Her hand dives into his shirt, reaching for her name still etched on his chest. He kisses her neck, sniffing in her fragrance. She does the same.

Just like old times.

His lips begin to track their way to hers, and then they meet. Politely at first. Like delicate paint strokes on a new canvas. And then it turns passionate. The kissing. It's like they're making up for all the distance, the time not spent together—everything, Arnika breaks from the kiss to breathe. Shadab still consumed by her presence darts back at her and is about to kiss Arnika's neck when she suddenly pushes him away.

'Arni?' A confused Shadab whispers. Arnika looks away.

'I'm sorry...I...I...can we drive to our spot? I need to talk to you.'

Shadab's confused. This doesn't make sense. He stays silent, hoping she'd say something. When the silence begins to stab, Shadab finally speaks.

'Arnika, are you okay?'

'Can we please go to our spot? Please Shadab.' She almost

pleads without looking at him.

'Umm... Sure.'

Awkward silence accompanies them till they reach a spot, which they used often to make out at, on the outskirts of the city. In peace.

After a quick scan for the cops, the car is stopped.

Arnika looks at the dying winter sun as she begins, not meeting his eyes, 'How have you been?'

He laughs uncomfortably.

'I'm confused... we drove all this way for this question?'

'Shadab...just answer me, please. How have you been?'

'What's up Arnika, you're scaring me now.' Shadab tries hard to joke but his voice betrays him.

'How have you been Shadab?' Arnika asks the same question again.

Irritated, Shadab snaps.

'As happy as I was before you decided to... What did you call it...oh yes, cool off...or as happy before you decided to suddenly stop me while we were you know... And now you're asking this weird question. I don't know Arnika. You tell me how should I be?'

She finally turns around and looks at him, taking his hand in hers.

'Shadab...look into my eyes. Please.'

The please melts the anger away and he does as instructed.

'You remember the first time we'd met? Princi's room,' she clears her throat and tries to imitate him. 'It's an iPod and not a MP3 player sir,' Shadab can't help but smile weakly. He has missed her so much. 'And then our first coffee...where was it?'

'Brick Bakers,' he whispers, still trying to ascertain where this conversation is going.

'Yes,' she leans over his shoulder. 'Brick Bakers...God...that cold coffee was so orgasmic…you saved me from those guys…the night you asked me out…in your boxers…wow!'

They both just look at each other. There's a moment of silence and then they burst out laughing.

'And then our first dinner date,' he begins.

'He was a pretty cute waiter,' she comments and he shoots a fake disgust look in her direction.

'And then our first kiss,' she whispers.

'The first of many,' he adds.

'The lists we made,' she continues.

'The shopping sagas…*A Walk to Remember*…man…did I sacrifice?' he grimaces.

'The cigarette stink. The times you didn't bother to brush your teeth,' she smiles weakly.

'What are you up to Arnika? Why are we discussing this? Please…'

Taking a deep breath ,she begins again. Her eyes moist.

'The fights once I went away… The drama…the pain…the heart ache…the fights, Shadab…the fights.'

'Arnikaaaa,' he groans, 'which relationship doesn't have problems? Which couple doesn't fight?'

'Did you notice something Shadab, all the beautiful memories that we have…so many of them… Don't you just love them? Don't you miss those times? The way we were… And now…the way we've become…'

He has nothing to say in reply. She continues. 'Shadab…only after we stopped talking did I realize something…in this last one month I missed you a lot… I missed us… the jokes, the random conversations, the hugs, the laughter, the warm dinners, the walks at the lake… goddamn I missed Shadab, my best friend… not just my boyfriend…'

He's confused at what she's trying to say, 'Believe me...it's been tough and when I say tough I mean as tough as finding a virgin in New York,' she laughs a mild laugh, looking at the sudden discomfort on his face. 'I know it's not been easy for you too,' she pulls his cheeks as his expressions fail to change.

'Please Arnika, we can work this out... I can... I mean, I promise I'll do better. Please give me another chance... just one more fucking chance... I'

'Let me finish, Shadab,' she interjects. 'I know you've sacrificed a lot for me... You've always been honest with me and that's what I love about you.'

A boulder hits the deepest pit inside his stomach. This is his moment to come clean, to make a new start, to let Arnika know that he slipped but he wants to stand up again. All these reasons and yet words fail Shadab. He knows he's being selfish. But he loves her and he can't let her go. Come what may. It's not him, these morals but it's him for now.

'Arnika I... I want to tell you something.'

'Yes?'

'Arnika...I...I...I love you.'

Arnika gives him a piercing look. Shadab doesn't want to face her right now. In this very moment he has realized his slip up would always be a secret in their relationship, he's too selfish to let her know and he's okay with it till it lets her stay.

Arnika comes close to him suddenly and places a peck on his cheek. Before Shadab can react, she begins.

'You're this amazing guy... if not the best boyfriend, definitely the best friend I could ever have. Now, please, don't interrupt me... I need to say this...' She takes his hands in hers. 'Shadab, you gave me the most meaningful and important relationship of my life... And I want that to be forever... And the only way it'll stay like that forever is by breaking up with you... It's over Shadab. It's over.'

Shadab just continues to stare at Arnika. After what seems like an eternity, he whispers.

'What? WHY?'

Arnika withdraws her hands. The hands that he was holding, all so tightly, just a second ago. She wipes a tear from her eye, even as another threatens to escape. She tries hard to compose herself, looking away from Shadab.

'I don't understand. You love our relationship and that's why you're ending it?'

Arnika takes a very long, deep breath, manages to compose herself and turns around to face him. This time with no expression on her face.

'Drop me home.'

Shadab cannot believe her. This isn't the Arnika he knows. His eyes try to search frantically for an answer in her eyes but all he gets is a distant look that shatters him from the inside.

'Drop me home.' She repeats, almost in a robotic tone.

In a daze, he powers the car into ignition. Opens his mouth to say something then shuts it again. He looks at her intently. There's no change in her expression. She's stoic, now looking ahead, not meeting his eye. Angrily, Shadab revs the car and drives back.

The drive back home has two constants. Silence and confusion. They finally reach Arnika's house.

Arnika looks at him for a moment before opening the car's door. He's lost. He just doesn't know what to say, or what to do?

'Arni'

She cuts him, placing a finger on his lips. She looks at him. He looks at her. Both pair of eyes welled up with emotion and salt. Suddenly Arnika begins to trace the same finger from his lips to his chin. It slithers along his neck and as she moves the collar of his shirt with her finger and that's when Shadab realizes where the finger is heading. The hickey.

'ARNIKA…I…I…'

'Shadab…pl…'

She can't control it anymore. She's tried too hard to be mature about this. Arnika bursts out crying. Shadab hugs her and she doesn't protest.

'I'm so sorry Arnika… it didn't mean anything… I swear I wanted to tell you but I was too scared of losing you… Please baby… we can put this behind us… I promise I'll do whatever you say…punish me…hit me… but please.'

Sobbing Arnika breaks free from his embrace. Shadab starts to plead again but she signals him to stop. She wipes her tears and looks at him.

'Shadab, yes I'm hurt… Not because you cheated on me, but because you hid this from me… It's not your fault… Honestly, I get it; people don't mean to cheat… And I wasn't even reasonable with you…but Shadab this just makes us realize one thing that we're really not in love… We're in love with the idea of being in it. Because when someone is in love, they're honest, they're not selfish. That's what we were…not what we are…I was selfish enough to block you from life, completely cut off. You were selfish enough to hide stuff from me. We both had our reasons. Perhaps, we're too young to figure out what love really means…and I understand that. I hope you too end up figuring it out. Thank you for all the beautiful memories. Let's keep it that way. My first love story… A lot like love, a li'l like chocolate.'

She opens the door of the car and gets down. Not looking back. Wiping her tears. But she knows she's done the right thing for both of them. She's not angry with him. She's not hurt. She understands what has happened. And knows in no time she will accept it too.

'Bye Shadab.' She whispers to herself as she opens the door of her house.

And that's the last time he sees her.

A Happy Ending?

And that's how it ends or does it?

1 August 2011

Days pass. Turn into weeks. Fly into months. Shadab begins his second year at college. Seven months after his breakup with Arnika, he's back at being what he was. A player.

And then that night, after he's come back from a random girl's apartment, he gets a message in Facebook.

From ARNIKA.

A person, who no longer exists in his friend list.

Errr hey!

Shadab, I knew what happened between Aastha and you, she'd messaged me on that day itself. I wouldn't have believed her, had I not seen the mark on your neck. That evening, believe me, it's okay…it's not your fault. We both knew it wasn't going to be easy in the first place. And we both cheated on each other…you physically and I, perhaps, emotionally by being selfish and not giving you enough time.

You must be wondering why I messaged you today after all these months.

Well Princess, I want your friendship back. I wanted to let you know that now I have Daksh in my life. Yes, I'm in a relationship again and today when we were discussing our past lives, I told him about you in full details and he coaxed me to message you. So here I am.

You have my number. Alisha told me. Text me when you're free.

What we shared was special. Is special. An almost love story. A lot like it.

Princess, don't be sad for it ended. Be happy for it lasted. I love you.

Your once-upon-a-time-humping prince.

Arnika

Acknowledgements

Just Friends happened and a lot of things changed. For the better. I got richer. My Facebook got messier. Love and chocolate happened. And, so, I decided to write the very book you're holding. And this definitely hasn't been a singular effort. A lot of people helped me intentionally and some, well, unintentionally.

Mom: Mrs Smiley Shahi, if I breathe, it is for you. If I cry, it is for you. If I strive, it is for you. If I pray, it is for you. And one day, if I fall and kiss the Earth goodbye, it will be for you.

Dad: Mr Sukhjit Shahi, for letting me take my own decisions and supporting them with a smile and lots of money.

Satvika, for letting me know what *A Lot Like Love... A Li'l Like Chocolate* means.

All my family and friends in Chandigarh and Pune (go SSLA!) for versing me with interesting situations, which I've definitely not taken into account in this book.

And in the end...YOU...for simply making me richer.

Happy reading. On the bed. Under it. In the toilet. On the pot. On the table. Okay... I shall stop.